Aidan

By

Ronna M. Bacon

ISBN 978-1-998821-29-7

Psalm 32:7 You are my hiding place; You preserve me from trouble; You surround me with songs of deliverance.

Phillipians 46-7 Be anxious for nothing, but in everything by prayer and supplication, with thanksgiving, let your requests be made known to God; and the peace of God, which surpasses all understanding, will guard your hearts and minds through Christ Jesus,

NKJV

Table of Contents

Chapter 1

Locking his vehicle, Aidan McNeill walked away from it, the hot late summer sun beating down on his black hair that was cropped slightly longer than the norm. His green eyes searched the area around him as he headed for a log cabin style restaurant before they raised to study the sky to the west. Dark clouds were moving in. With the mugginess in the air, Aidan fully expected a thunderstorm at the very least later that day.

Aidan was on a well-deserved vacation and didn't want to be there. His friends had been through life and death adventures in the last couple of years. Working on them had stressed him past where he knew that he was burnt out and had to walk away. Lyle, the chief detective, had given him no option, simply telling him to walk away from the office and not come back for a week. And then Lyle had asked that he stay out of trouble, a slight grin on his face. Toryn, the police chief of Oak City and a good friend of Aidan's, had echoed that sentiment. Toryn and his wife, Slaney, had just come through a life-threatening adventure that had affected the police department in an unwanted way.

Pulling open the old-fashioned screen door, Aidan stepped into the restaurant, blinking for a moment to let his eyes adjust to the dimness after the bright sun outside. There were only a few customers in the building, their eyes almost glaring at him for disturbing them. He shrugged and walked to a table near the back of the building, sitting with his back to

—

7

the wall and where he could watch the others. This was common for Aidan to do.

Shivering slightly, Aidan felt a sense of danger in the building. He just didn't know why. And one thing that he had learned while a police officer had been to respect those feelings. They had saved his life more than once.

His meal finished, Aidan felt the sense of danger growing even more. Most of the customers had left. The only one remaining was a young lady, around his age he decided, who sat at a table nearby. Aidan was on his feet, his coffee mug in his hand, as he moved to sit at her table. She looked up startled for a moment and then frowned at him.

"I'm sorry. I didn't mean to startle you." Aidan looked around, not seeing any serving staff or anyone else for that matter. "I feel danger in here. Would you come with me? I'm Aidan McNeill, a detective for Oak City." He studied her, taking in the deep red curls that brushed her shoulders and the brown eyes that held fear and apprehension. He became determined to find out what just why that was. His identification was out for Artis to study before he tucked it away in his pocket.

"Hi. I'm Artis Aislinn. I'm sorry. I don't know why you would say that." Artis looked around, her hands gripping her mug tighter.

"There is something or someone here that means you harm." Aidan was on his feet, money dropped to the table to pay for their meals, before he reached for her hand and pulled her with him.

Artis didn't protest at Aidan's moves. She had learned to trust her instincts and her instincts were telling her to trust Aidan. God was also speaking to her heart, giving her the peace that she needed at the moment. Things had not been normal for Artis lately and that had been worrying her. Her work as a youth protection worker was hectic and dangerous at times. She had needed a break and taken off for some time alone. Only, that didn't seem to be happening at the moment.

Aidan tugged at Artis, pulling her in a more rapid movement towards his truck. He searched the area, feeling someone out there and not sure where they were.

"Where's your car?" Aidan was puzzled as he could only see his in the parking lot. Not even a car that would belong to a worker remained. That spurred him to pick up his pace.

"I walked. I'm staying close by." Artis looked around. "Someone is out there. Where are they?"

"I don't know." Aidan shot a quick glance over his shoulder as he felt Artis tugging him to a stop. "What are you stopping us for?" He faced forward, momentarily dismayed at the men standing in front of them. Then his police training kicked in and he tucked away as much information about the men as he could for future reference. "Who are you?" His feet stopped as if he had hit a brick wall. He could hear a whimper from Artis and looked briefly at her.

Artis was staring at the men in front of them. She thought that she knew one of them but fear had taken

—

over her mind. She spun as much as she could to look around her, seeing the men behind them. She could feel Aidan's hand tightening on hers before he reluctantly tugged her forward towards his truck. She was shoved into the back seat as he was forced behind the wheel.

"Where are we going?" Aidan stared at the man seated beside him. So far, none of the men had spoken.

"Turn left and head that way." The man's words were clipped and harsh sounding.

Aidan shared a look with Artis in the rearview mirror before he did as was ordered. Twenty minutes later, he was directed to pull to the side of the road and turn off the truck. He did as he was ordered and then dropped down to the ground, reaching for Artis' hand as she was shoved out of the back seat.

Forced to walk forward into the trees, Aidan kept watch for a way to escape. There was none. He felt the first drops of rain as they fell and began to worry about Artis. He shrugged out of his sweatshirt, knowing that he could not wear it and see Artis wet and cold. Aidan hadn't meant to wear it that day but habit had him reaching for it. He would wear them to hide his weapon when he was on duty.

A hand landing harshly on his shoulder stopped him abruptly. He could hear faint conversation from behind him before they were forced into a cave and to the back of it. Aidan turned to face the men, tucking Artis behind him. He frowned as he saw the men approaching and then standing in front of them.

Aidan remained silent, his eyes steady on the man he had pegged as the leader. He didn't know them. All he knew was that God had spoken to him and told him that he had to protect Artis. He didn't need a reason why or to hear an audible voice to know that God had spoken to him. Aidan could feel Artis' fingers digging into his back as she gripped his T-shirt. Artis was afraid and rightly so. Her prayers didn't seem to be rising past the ceiling of the cave.

Aidan's body flew backwards as a weapon discharged. He landed heavily, taking Artis down with him. Artis screamed and scrambled away from him, shaken by the force with which she hit the rock floor. She stared in horror at the men and then at Aidan. She scrambled towards him, a hand reaching for the bloody furrow that creased the side of his head.

"Why? What did he do to you?" She spun on her knees to face the men, tears of fear on her face.

The man pointed his weapon at her before he raised it and discharged it once more. Artis screamed and huddled against Aidan as shards of rock showered down on the arms that she had wrapped around her head. He then turned and walked away. She heard sounds at the cave entrance but was too terrified to look. Raising her head, Artis' attention was on Aidan. He was alive, she knew, but hurt. And she had no way to help him other than using his sweatshirt to try and stem the flow of blood from his wound.

The cave was dark and damp. Artis shivered as she became more aware of her surroundings. On her feet, she searched for a way out, stopping at the entrance. It had been blocked and she didn't have the strength to move the branches that were piled there. A sob rose within her as she looked up, begging God for help. He was there with them, she knew. She just prayed for someone human to come along and rescue them.

Artis returned to Aidan's side, a hand on his chest. It was still rising and falling. She felt relief that he was alive. He needed medical attention, she knew. She just didn't know how to get that for him.

—

Chapter 2

It was early evening when Artis roused once more. She had sat for the remainder of the afternoon with one hand on Aidan's, the other arm wrapped around herself in an attempt to keep warm. That had not worked out as well as she had thought it would.

Artis rose and stretched, her eyes on the entrance to the cave. The sun was setting, that much was obvious through the holes where the branches didn't completely conceal the outdoors. She walked as quietly as she could towards it, a frown on her face. She had no idea who the men were or what they wanted. She paused and turned to look at Aidan before she shrugged. Perhaps he was the one that they were after. Artis had full intentions of asking the men that when they reappeared. And they would reappear, she was certain of that. They always did, unless they wanted the captives to die. She paled at that thought. *God? Are You here? Do You plan for us to die in this cave? Somehow that's not what I want. I know. I know. You're in control. And You have plans that we don't know about. I just don't have to like it, now do I?* Artis was not being disrespectful. She was just talking to God as her Abba Father, her Daddy. That was how she had been taught to pray, to bring every feeling that she had to God.

Pausing at the entrance, Artis tentatively touched the branches. She could remove them, she decided, but something kept her from doing that. She could hear faint movement outside and sighed. Some of the men were still there. She wanted to know why she and Aidan had been kidnapped and why he had been shot. It didn't make sense to her, not at the moment. And one thing that Artis hated was for things not to make sense.

Artis turned away from the entrance and then did a more thorough search of the cave. She frowned as she felt an empty space in the wall. Turning quickly to search the entrance, she pulled out her phone and found the flashlight on it. Shining the light into the space, Artis felt hopeful for a moment. Perhaps this was a way out for them. That was, if she could get Aidan on his feet. If he ever roused, that was. He hadn't over the afternoon and that scared her. Not much scare Artis any more, not given her work.

Sitting back down beside Aidan, Artis prayed for him. She was worried, she had to admit, that his injury was serious. It more than likely was, she decided, as she gently lifted the sweatshirt from the injury. It had stopped bleeding but it would start up again at some point. Artis worked to tear a strip of material from the shirt and then tied it as tightly as she thought was necessary around Aidan's head. Her hand rested against his cheek for a moment.

Aidan's eyes began to flicker as he fought to regain his wits, as Artis told him afterwards. His eyes opened but didn't focus. He frowned at the pain that he felt and then at the lady's voice begging him to awaken. He lost that fight and dropped into that dark well that seemed waiting for him. He didn't hear the fear-choked voice of Artis as she begged him to awaken, that she needed him to. She had found a way out, she told him in a whisper. Only he needed to be awake and on his feet for them to escape.

Artis gave up at last and settled more closely to Aidan. She felt protected by him even though he was unconscious. She slept at last, her head drooping down as she sat beside the detective. Neither heard the movement at the entrance of the cave when the branches were removed or the quiet footsteps that approached them.

Gentle hands moved Artis away from Aidan and then gathered her into strong arms to carry her from her captivity. The man heard the low murmur that Aidan was hurt and needed her. She couldn't leave him.

A second man gently lifted Aidan to his feet and then draped him over his shoulders before he was carried from the cave. He was laid down for a few moments as the branches were once more carefully and quietly replaced in the entrance. The two men stared at it and then at the three men who were sound asleep and hadn't heard their quiet movements. The two men headed away as rapidly as they felt they could, finding the skiff that they had tied up to a tree on the bank of the nearby river. The two captives were placed as comfortably as they could be before the two men were in and oars were in their hands. A quick shove off from the bank sent the skiff on its way up river from the cave.

Rousing in the morning, the three men rose and stretched, confident that their captives were still alive and in the cave. Their instructions had been to keep

---

them there and then in the morning transfer them to the van that would be waiting at the foot of the hill.

The older man threw aside the branches and stood into the cave, pausing as he didn't see the two. Consternation was great on their faces as they realized that the couple was no longer there. Blame was placed on each other as they sought to find them and couldn't. The men were puzzled by their disappearance and fled the cave as rapidly as they could. Something sinister and mysterious had happened overnight and they no longer wanted to be part of it. They just kept running until they found their lodgings. Gathering their belongings, they fled the village and just kept going, separating as they reached a large town.

The two men who had rescued the couple spoke quietly to one another before they turned from the cabin and headed for a vehicle. They were after Aidan's truck, needing to move it back to where he had been staying.

"You're sure about this?" The younger man spoke at last, breaking the silence in the cab of the truck.

The older man shrugged.

"I'm not but it's what we're to do. He has a reason for that." He pulled to a stop beside Aidan's truck. "You have his keys?" The younger man nodded. "Okay, then. I'll follow you to where he was staying."

An hour later, the men were back and preparing a meal for them all. The older man, Gabe by name, had paused for a moment before he headed to stand and study Artis. She didn't seem to have moved. He nodded before he headed for Aidan. This time, Gabe bent over Aidan, assessing him and then changing out the bandage that surrounded his head. He was able to place a smaller one that covered the wound. He was not satisfied that either one of the couple had not roused. That would happen, he knew. He just needed them on their feet so that he could return them to where Aidan was staying.

Mike turned from where he had set down their plate, a question on his face.

"Are they awake?"

Gabe shook his head.

"No, they're not. She will be shortly." Gabe hesitated for a moment. "We'll need to talk with them, Mike. I'm not sure that they'll like what we have to say."

Three hours later, Artis began to awaken. She felt the blanket before her eyes opened. She stared around the room, a frown on her face. Artis shoved back the blankets and rose, finding clean clothing waiting for her. She fingered them before she hunted for the bathroom and a shower.

Dressed in the clean clothes, Artis paused with a hand on the door. Her head bowed as she prayed for whatever it was that she would find once she opened it. Stepping out into the living area of the cabin, Artis paused once more, searching for someone. She just didn't know who. A sound had her spinning to search for the source. Seeing someone lying on the couch, Artis moved slowly forward, not sure what she would find.

On her knees, Artis' hand rested on Aidan's cheek before she reached for his head to touch the bandage. He moved restlessly under his touch until his hand reached to grasp hers that rested on his chest. Aidan tried to rouse, to reach up through the dark tunnel that seemed to be drawing him down deeper and deeper into it. He heard a lady's voice speaking with him but he just could not understand what her words were.

Artis was frightened when she could not rouse Aidan. She also could not remove her hand from his, his grip was just that tight. Hearing footsteps behind her, Artis gave a small scream as she jumped and then spun as much as she could.

"Who are you?" Artis' eyes were huge as she stared at Gabe.

"My name's Gabe. Mike and I rescued you two last night. Your man is hurt."

Artis was shaking her head even as she heard his words. Aidan was not her man. Not a chance, she decided. She was destined to be single until she died. To be married and be a wife and mother was a dream that she had buried deep into her heart. God knew her dream but so far, that had not come to fruition.

"I'm sorry. I don't know you." Her voice wavered slightly before she tried her best to steady it.

"No, you don't." Gabe's hand helped her to her feet and to a chair at the table. "Come and eat something. I doubt that you had any food in the last few hours." He gave a grin as she shook her head. "We won't hurt you. We found you in the cave and brought you here. We want to help you."

"You do? You don't know me or Aidan." Artis reached for the glass of water, hating that her hand was shaking.

"We do know of you both. Someone is looking out for you. For both of you." Gabe had a sympathetic to her plight. "I don't know why you were taken captive but we do need to get you back to your home."

Artis nodded, knowing that was true. She had to go home. Only, she didn't want to. Artis had put in her resignation to her office and was as they say footloose. She was looking for a new town. Her eyes turned in a thoughtful way towards Aidan. Perhaps his town would work. She had looked into opportunities there and had planned on heading that way. Now, she had a reason to do so. Artis felt that she needed to make sure that Aidan healed from his injury.

Aidan roused at last, hearing a voice calling his name. His head twisted before pain stopped the movement. His hand found the side of his head, pain intensifying for a moment.

"Aidan?" Artis' voice was low, begging him to wake up.

"Where am I?" Aidan finally looked, not recognizing the cabin before his eyes stopped on Artis. "Do I know you?"

"I'm Artis. You tried to help me yesterday. Only we were kidnapped and stuffed into a cave. Two men rescued us. I just don't remember that." She was unable to stop the tears that welled up and trickled down her cheeks.

Aidan shifted enough so that he could wipe the tears from her cheeks.

"I'm sorry that happened, Artis, is it?" At her nod, he shifted again, this time to shove himself to a sitting position. He wasn't sure what she meant but he sensed that she had spoken the truth. "Tell me what happened."

Artis finally nodded, telling him what happened to them. She just could not explain how they had escaped.

"They blocked the entrance?" At her nod, Aidan's head dropped forward. He was having trouble thinking through what she had said. He wanted to be in his office to search for their kidnappers. Only he had no idea where his truck was. Aidan also knew that he was not able to drive as yet, not with his head aching as much as it was. "What happened to me?"

"They just shot you, Aidan. I was so worried about you. It didn't make sense with them shooting you." Artis shifted herself to sit on the floor, her hand still tight in Aidan's. Neither of them made a move to release it.

"Why? Did they say anything?"

Artis shook her head, turning to look at Gabe as he walked towards them.

"Gabe?"

"Artis? You're okay?" His attention turned to Aidan. "Aidan? May I call you that?" Aidan nodded as Gabe took in a deep breath. "We need to get you home, Aidan. Your truck is where you were staying. Artis? Your car?"

"It's at the cabin where I was staying. Where are you planning on taking us?" Artis didn't want to leave Aidan and she felt his hand tighten on hers. Obviously, he didn't want to leave her either.

"You are in danger, Artis. Why? I don't know. Aidan is collateral damage to that." Gabe heard Mike coming up behind him. "We are going to take you to your cabin, Artis. Mike here will drive your car to where we're going. Aidan? You're not able to drive or be on your own. We'll stop and have you assessed.

However, you want to protect Artis and we need to figure out how you do that."

Aidan had drawn in a deep breath as Gabe had been speaking. He knew what Gabe meant. He wasn't able to be on his own. His family was not in Oak City, away for a few days on vacation, or so he thought. They would come if he needed them. Aidan just didn't want to leave Artis on her own. He knew nothing about her but he felt God's nudge to do something to protect her.

"Artis?" Aidan waited until Artis looked at him. "We don't know each other. But I would like to offer you my name until we sort this out. Marry me and then we'll work this through. I am a police detective and have resources to help do that."

Artis stared at him in shock. This was not what she had expected, not at all. She glanced at Gabe and saw his nod and then looked at Mike, who simply stood and watched them before he walked away and out of the cabin. Danger was approaching them, he could tell, and he wanted them out of there.

Chapter 4

Aidan slumped in the passenger seat of his truck, knowing that Gabe was heading for a hospital to have him assessed. He turned his head slightly to watch Artis who sat behind Gabe. Her eyes were on him, a puzzled look in them. He sighed to himself. This is not how his week was to have gone.

"Aidan? Here. Let's get that head of yours looked at." Gabe was out of the truck and around to help Aidan down to the ground.

Aidan gave a groan as his feet hit the pavement in front of the small hospital. He felt Artis' hand in his and he tightened his grip. Gabe's hand under his arm helped him walk through the doors and then to a room where he stretched out on a gurney. Aidan refused to let go of Artis' hand despite her tugging at his grip.

Two hours later, Gabe once more helped Aidan back into the truck, this time to the back seat at his request. Artis sat close to him, her arm wrapped around his. His assessment had been better than they expected. Aidan did have a concussion and it would take time for him to recover physically. It was the emotional and mental recovery that would take time.

Aidan unlocked the door to his home, stepping into it and then reaching for Artis' hand. He was unsure what to say or what to do other than to walk her through the house.

Artis was hesitant to walk through Aidan's home. It appeared that it was now theirs. Gabe had surprised them by stating that he was a minister and would marry them, if they were willing to do that. He could not see any other way for them at present.

Aidan had prayed for Artis as they had stared at one another. He was willing to take that step, knowing that others of his friends had done that. He was just not sure that it was the way that they should take. Artis had finally nodded, not having felt God stopping her. She had no idea where it would go from there but she was trusting Aidan in a way that she had never trusted anyone before.

Late that afternoon, Aidan stood in the kitchen, staring into the fridge. Mike had done a food run for them, bringing in what they would need for the next few days. Aidan had not stocked up before he left, knowing that he would be away for a week. He turned and walked to his front door, stepping out on the front porch and staring around. A friend had taken care of the yard work for him and he was grateful for that. Aidan heard footsteps beside him and he reached to wrap an arm around her. Artis was not sure of what to say or how to feel. Aidan made her feel safe and wanted

"Aidan? How is your head?" Artis looked up at him, marvelling at how tall he was.

"It's hurting but not as bad as it was. I'll see the police department physician tomorrow. I'll need you to drive me, however." Aidan looked down at her, seeing the struggles that she was going through.

"I can do that. I'm not working at the moment. I think I told you that I work as a youth protection officer."

"You did. What are your plans, then? I know that there are openings here if you're interested."

Artis nodded, knowing that Aidan was trying to take care of her.

"I'll think about it. I'm just not sure that I will stay in this town. This marriage is only temporary." She walked away from him and back into the house.

Aidan watched her walk away from him before he studied the engraved rose gold ring on his finger. This was not how he had planned to marry, if he even had done that. He just could not walk away from Artis. Aidan had trusted Gabe when he suggested that deed but he was now having doubts.

Looking up as he heard a car door shut, Aidan sighed. Lyle, his supervisor, was walking towards him.

"Aidan? What are you doing home? You planned to be away for the week?" Lyle studied the younger man. "And just what did you go and do?"

"I am home, Lyle, and we need to talk. I was shot trying to protect someone. I have no idea who the men were. And Artis doesn't either." Aidan hesitated for a moment, praying for his lady, before he turned towards the house.

"Aidan. Wait. What are you talking about?" Lyle's hand on Aidan's arm stopped him.

Aidan paused, knowing that he had to confess what had happened. He just wasn't sure how to.

Lyle's eyes raised to the door where he saw Artis waiting for Aidan. He frowned, not knowing the lady. He turned back to Aidan, seeing him watching Artis.

"Aidan? Who is this lady?"

"This is Artis." Aidan reached for Artis and drew her into his arms. "She's my bride, Lyle. We married earlier today. It's to protect Artis. We're still talking through what we know." Aidan swayed on his feet, sudden pain driving him to his knees, taking Artis down with him.

Artis spun on her knees and was then on her feet, attempting to draw Aidan up on his. Lyle gave an inaudible exclamation and then had lifted Aidan to his feet and manhandled him through the door and to the couch where he gently shoved Aidan down.

Aidan gave a groan before his eyes slid closed. Lyle and Artis' voices faded as he lost consciousness. Lyle shifted Aidan to a lying position on the couch, Artis on her knees beside it.

"Artis? What happened to Aidan?" Lyle waited for Artis to speak.

"He was shot trying to protect me yesterday. We did have him seen at a hospital on our way back here." Artis looked up at Lyle, seeing the disbelief on his face. "It happened just as I said. We were kidnapped from a diner, shoved into a cave and left there with the entrance blocked, and then woke up in a cabin with our rescuers. They got us back here. Now, what are we to do with Aidan?"

Lyle had his phone out, calling for help. He walked back to the living room doorway and watched Artis as she sat with an arm across Aidan's chest. Something was going on there, he decided, something that he had seen too many times in the past. Lyle looked down at his phone, knowing that he had another call to make.

"Toryn?" Lyle turned to walk back outside of the house, passing the paramedics as they walked towards the house. "Aidan's home."

"He is?" Toryn, the police chief of the town, turned from his back deck. It was Saturaday and he and Slaney had enjoyed their lunch out there. "He shouldn't be. Is he okay?"

"No, he's not. He was shot, the bullet creasing the side of his head. I have paramedics here to take him in to be assessed again."

"Shot? How?" Toryn reached for Slaney's hand as she moved with him towards the door. "Where is he?"

"He's at home right now but he'll be heading for the hospital." Lyle stepped back into the house and stopped beside Artis. He could see the distress on her face and simply wrapped an arm around her, causing her to jump. She wasn't used to that. "There's a story there. The thing is, Toryn, that he stepped in and married a beautiful lady to save her." Lyle held the phone away from his ear, causing Artis to stare at him in disbelief. "That's what I said. I haven't gotten the

---

whole story yet. Aidan collapsed just after I got here. I came at his request." Lyle walked out of the house following the stretcher bearing Aidan and locked the door behind him.

"Okay. Slaney and I are on our way to the hospital. Call me when you get there." Toryn turned to Slaney, seeing the same shock on her face that was on his. "Slaney?"

"Toryn? Did I hear Lyle correctly? Aidan's married?" This was not what either one of them had expected to hear. "That's not Aidan."

"No, it's not. But he would step in if he felt it necessary. But he would only do that if he knew that it was God's plan."

"That's true." Slaney stared down at her phone. "I'm calling Gideon. He needs to be there."

Toryn simply nodded, his thoughts on his friend. *Lord, heal my friend. Don't let him go through the life and death struggles that Slaney and I did. I don't know that our force could take this right now, not after losing two colleagues not that long ago.*

Chapter 5

His hand on her right arm, Lyle walked Artis through the doors of the ambulance bay, following the stretcher. He paused for a moment, knowing that the medical staff needed to assess Aidan. He also knew that Artis would not take kindly to being separated from him. Lyle sighed and directed her to the room where they would find Aidan.

The medical staff looked askance at Artis and then at Lyle, finding him just nodding. Artis stopped short of the stretcher, knowing that she could not be as close to Aidan as she wanted to be.

Lyle turned as the charge nurse stopped beside him, a frown on her face. He sighed once more.

"Lyle? Who is she?" Beth nodded towards Artis.

"It's a long story, Beth, which I don't know the full details for. Aidan is married and this is his bride, Artis. We'll need to add her as his next of kin."

"He is? That's quite the surprise." Lyle watched Artis closely. "I'll move her to the waiting room soon. For now, she needs to be with him."

"I see. It should be okay." Beth looked around. "Where's Toryn?"

"Likely in the waiting room. I spoke with him not that long ago." Aidan moved to stand beside Artis. "Artis? We'll need to wait outside. Come on. I'm not leaving you."

Artis nodded, reaching for a moment to grasp Aidan's hand, not finding him responding. She drew in a wavering breath and turned to walk away with Lyle. Artis found a seat in the waiting room where she could watch the door, knowing that she would be back through them as soon as she could.

Toryn and Slaney paused just as they stepped into the waiting room, searching for Lyle. Lyle waited for a moment, his eyes on Artis, before he walked over to stand beside Toryn. Slaney searched his face and then moved to sit beside Artis, startling that lady.

"I'm sorry. Do I know you?" Artis had her arms wrapped around herself, worry for Aidan uppermost in her mind.

"No, we've never been introduced. I'm a friend of Aidan's. My name is Slaney. Toryn is a good friend of Aidan's." Slaney simply reached to hug Artis, not finding her responding.

"I see. Aidan mentioned you." Artis kept her eyes on the door. "It's taking a long time."

"It does take a while. They will need to do imaging as well. Are you okay?" Slaney was worried about her new friend.

Artis shrugged. She had no idea how she was to feel. Her whole world had been turned upside down in the last twenty-four hours or so. God was in control, she knew. She just wished that He would share His plans for her life. She had not thought that it would include marrying someone as she had, especially not a police officer.

Toryn searched Lyle's face for a moment before he too looked towards Artis. This was not Aidan, he knew, to do this. Aidan never dated and generally took care in how he approached the ladies.

"Lyle? What do you know?"

"Not a lot. Other than introducing me to Artis and telling me that they were married, he didn't get a chance to say much. He collapsed not long after I got there." Lyle was worried about his detective. Aidan was the best one that he had on his squad. Right now, they had a number of cases under investigation and he really couldn't lose Aidan.

"I see. Introduce me to the lady, Lyle. We'll talk with her and see what we can find out. Where's George?" George was another detective who usually worked closely with Aidan. Toryn looked around for him, not seeing him in the busy waiting room.

"He's on the scene of that fire and homicide." Lyle was concerned about George. He was bearing the work of two while Aidan was away and now this? This would compound that.

Lyle paused beside Artis before his hand rested on her shoulder. He felt her jump and then shift to look at him. A frown was on her face.

Toryn crouched down beside Artis, compassion on his face. He studied her before he looked over at Slaney, who shook her head. Another one who is hard to read, he decided. *Lord, we'll need Your help on this one.*

"Artis, this is Toryn Knight. He is our police chief. More importantly, he is Aidan's good friend. Slaney and he are married. They will not walk away from you. Toryn, this is Artis. She is Aidan's bride. I don't know the story of what happened as yet, but we'll find out."

Toryn nodded, not taking his eyes from Artis. Artis stared back at him, not sure what to say or how to react.

"Artis? Have you been back with Aidan?" At her nod, he looked up at Lyle and then Slaney. "We'll get you back in a bit. Beth, the charge nurse, will come looking for you. Lyle or I will go with you. Now, what can you tell me about what happened?"

"Aidan tried to protect me yesterday. We were kidnapped just after we left the diner. It was strange. There was no one left in the diner and only Aidan's truck in the parking lot. We were stopped in the parking lot of the diner and forced into Aidan's vehicle. A short while later, we were forced into a cave. Aidan stood in front of me and that's when they shot him. I don't think that they meant to kill him. They blocked the entrance with branches, preventing from getting out. I think that men were there as I thought I heard their voices. I did what I could to help Aidan before I slept and when I woke up, we were in a cabin. A man by the name of Gabe looked after us. There was a man named Mike who helped him. We stopped at a hospital where Aidan was seen. Gabe suggested that we should marry to protect me. I'm not sure that we made the right choice. He was hurt because of me."

—

"We'll look into it more. Lyle or George, another one of our investigators, will speak with you." Toryn looked up as Beth approached. He rose, his hand out to draw Artis to her feet. "Here. Off you go with Beth to find Aidan. Lyle will go with you."

Artis nodded, her emotions too raw for her to speak. She walked away, Lyle's hand under her arm to steady her, heading for her groom, not sure what she would find.

Toryn and Slaney watched her walk away, Toryn's arm around his wife. He had seen too many of his friends go through adventures as they were called. Slaney leaned against Toryn, drawing from his strength.

"What can we do for her, Toryn?" Slaney was very concerned about Artis.

"I don't know, Slaney. We'll see what we need to do for her. I don't think that she's from our town."

"I don't think she is." Slaney felt eyes on her and looked around, frowning at the two men who stood near the entrance door. "Toryn, do you know those men?"

Toryn looked around and shook his head. He turned to walk towards them and found that they had disappeared. He frowned. He walked rapidly to the outside, not seeing them. That puzzled Toryn. The men had disappeared far too quickly.

—

Chapter 6

Artis curled up in a chair that evening, her eyes closing as she prayed and then slept. She had been taught to pray about everything. She just wanted her mother and father right then. Only they were out of the country on a business trip for her mother and would not be back for at least two weeks. She had sent off an email to them, letting them know what had happened. Emails were difficult to retrieve at times, she knew, in the country where they were.

George had appeared not that long before. He had stared at Lyle, not sure that he had heard him correctly.

"I'm sorry. You said that this is Aidan's wife? I didn't know that he was dating anyone." George positioned himself just inside Aidan's room to study Artis.

"It's a story in itself, George. Unfortunately, Aidan hasn't been awake long enough for me to speak with him. They're keeping him here tonight and then sending him home. Aidan's off on one of the adventures that we told Toryn ended with him." Lyle gave a quick grin for a moment in response to George's grin. "Artis has not been able to tell us much other than what happened. She didn't recognize the men. However, she did state that Aidan seemed to sense danger and had moved her from the diner and was trying to get away with her. She's been watched carefully from the sounds of it."

"What is her occupation?" George turned to watch Aidan, seeing that Aidan was becoming restless.

"She's a youth protection worker. She tells me that she just quit her job in her town and was planning on moving towns." Lyle shrugged as George looked at him.

"A youth protection worker? That could explain it." George pulled out his notepad and made some notes. "Do you know what organization that she worked for"

"I do. I left that information on your desk." Lyle walked towards the bed, finding Aidan with his eyes open although they were clouded with pain. "Aidan?"

"Lyle? Where am I?" Aidan was also confused, not recognizing that he was in a hospital room.

Lyle sighed. *Thanks, Lord, for letting me tell him. He's not going to take it well.*

"You were shot yesterday, Aidan. Now, you're in the hospital." Lyle's hand rested on Aidan's shoulder to keep him in his bed.

"Shot? How? Did we get the assailant?" Aidan's head was twisting until he saw Artis. His restless movements stopped and he waited for her to awaken. "Who's this?"

"This is Artis, Aidan. Apparently you two were married today." Lyle bit back his smile as Aidan continued to stare at Artis.

"No, we didn't. I wasn't dating anyone. I would remember her." Aidan finally looked at the two men, seeing Lyle nodding. "Explain, Lyle. I want to know what you know."

"And I don't know a lot, Aidan. Apparently, yesterday you rescued Artis from danger, ended up kidnapped, were shot, and then rescued. Your rescuer suggested that you marry to protect her and you did. He was a minister. We just have not found him to verify anything." Lyle smiled at Aidan, a sad smile that held compassion for him.

"We did? I don't remember." Aidan's head went back on the pillow, his eyes closing as he slept.

Lyle turned away, studying Artis. He wasn't sure if she was still asleep or just pretending to be. He would question her in the morning. He walked away, heading for his home, leaving George in the waiting room to work through what he could. The next day was Sunday. Lyle had every intention of speaking with Gideon, their minister, and sending him to speak with Aidan and Artis.

Artis looked around, distress on her face. Aidan's friends seemed to doubt their story. Aidan couldn't remember it. She wanted to run but knew that she couldn't. If she ran, Aidan would come after her and he wasn't fit enough to do that. She paced at last, stopping at the bedside, a hand resting on Aidan's shoulder.

Aidan jumped at her touch and then his eye sprung open. He stared around, his gaze finding Artis as she stood with her head bowed and her eyes closed. A single tear trickled down her cheek. Aidan shifted until he could sit upright despite the headache that worsened. His finger reached to wrap away the tear before he simply wrapped her into his arms. Startled, Artis jumped before she relaxed against him. She felt safe with Aidan and couldn't understand why.

"Are you okay?" Aidan's voice was kept low. He knew that an officer would be at the door and he didn't want him or her to enter until he had determined if this lady who was his bride had been soothed.

Artis shook her head. She was not okay and hadn't been for a while, she realized. She leaned back to look at Aidan, seeing the pain on his face but also his determination to protect her.

"Aidan? How are you?"

Aidan shrugged, not sure how to respond. His head was aching but not quite as bad as it had been. He was just so worried about his lady. Aidan frowned, not remembering the ceremony where she became his bride. And he should.

"I'm okay. Can I leave?" Aidan wanted out of there to start his investigation. He just didn't think that it would happen at that moment.

"Not until the morning. They want to reassess you at that point. And I won't let you leave." Artis moved out of Aidan's arms, feeling bereft for a moment. "Do you remember anything?"

Aidan shook his head and regretted it. His eyes squeezed shut against the stab of pain that shot through it from temple to temple. He felt a gentle hand on his cheek and turned into it. Squinting, Aidan turned to Artis, seeing the concern on her face. He sank back once more on the pillow, knowing that he had to rest and not wanting to. He wanted to be out hunting for whoever had done this to him and also hunting for whoever it was that was after his lady.

His phone chiming caught his attention. It was the tone that he used for his mother. Squinting harder, he frowned at the message. It simply stated that they knew that he was in difficulty and were on their way home, arriving in the middle of the night. He sighed. Aidan would need to introduce them to Artis. Only he had no way to explain what had happened. His eyes closed and he slept, leaving Artis to watch over night for him.

Chapter 7

Aidan walked slowly into his home, Artis linking her arm with his to steady him. Toryn and Slaney followed, electing to skip church that morning and spend that time with their friends. Slaney moved towards the kitchen, depositing the bags that she held onto the countertop before she turned and stood watching Aidan.

Artis was frustrated. She was insisting that Aidan needed to be in bed to rest. He, on the other hand, was insisting that he be in his office. He needed to start an investigation. Toryn watched the battle between the couple before he spoke up.

"Aida, first you need to get cleaned up and into clean clothes." Toryn turned Aidan towards his bedroom.

Artis watched closely, knowing that Toryn was correct but she also knew that Aidan would want to do just what he said. How did she prevent that?

Slaney wrapped an arm around her friend and turned her towards her bedroom. She stood watching Artis for a moment before she was away to the kitchen and back with a bag.

"Here, Artis. You need to clean up as well. Here are some new clothes for you as well as some shampoo and body wash. It's our gift to you." Slaney reached to hug her new friend. "Go on. I'll work on a meal for us. It's what we do for our friends."

Artis turned to study Slaney, hope in her heart. *Is this You, Lord? Are You providing friends for me here in this new town?*

Thirty minutes later, Aidan sank gratefully into his easy chair, his eyes closing for a moment against the sudden stab of pain from his wound. He had been warned about overdoing it and had done just that in taking his shower and dressing in clean clothes. Aidan felt Artis' hand on his arm as she sank to the ottoman beside his chair.

"Aidan? You overdid it." Artis was highly worried about him.

"I did, but I had to. I need to start investigating this." Aidan's eyes closed for a moment. *Lord, I can't do this. I need to protect my lady and I just can't do this.*

"Not at the moment. You know what the doctor said. You need to rest. You can't use the computer for a few days." Artis was frustrated at Aidan's unwillingness to take it easy.

Aidan opened his eyes to study the beautiful lady sitting beside him. He was still in awe that they were married. He just wished that he could remember that. It wasn't fair to her that he didn't.

"Artis? Where is your family?" Slaney sat close by, curious as Artis had not mentioned them.

"They're overseas right now for Mom's work. I can't reach them by phone, only email. I sent an email yesterday but I don't know when they'll retrieve it. If they do, they'll be home as soon as they can." Artis refused to let the tears that clouded her vision fall. She felt that she had cried enough over the last twenty-four hours.

"Okay. We'll watch for that then. Aidan? Your parents?" Slaney turned next to Aidan, intruding into his thoughts.

"Mom and Dad? They should have landed this morning in Toronto and are on their way here. At least, that was their plan. They'll stop at their house first and get situated away before heading here." Aidan squinted at the clock on the fireplace mantle. "I would expect them here at any time."

Toryn was on his feet, heading for the front door. He had heard a vehicle stop outside and was concerned that it would be someone meaning Aidan and Artis harm. He stopped before moving forward to hug Aidan's parents. Toryn had always been treated as another son by them, knowing them he decided as long as he could remember.

"Alin? Ardeen? You're home. Aidan does need you." Toryn hesitated, biting at his lip.

"Toryn? You're troubled." Ardeen studied her son's friend. "Can you tell us or should we wait for Aidan to confess?"

Toryn grinned for a moment, knowing that Ardeen had read him correctly.

"I am. And I think it is best that Aidan confess. Although to tell you the truth, he's not likely to tell you much." Toryn hesitated, not wanting to say much more.

—

"We'll see then, won't we, Toryn?" Alin was familiar enough to know that Toryn was conflicted. "He said that he had been injured. How is he?"

Toryn nodded, glad to have something that he could say. As the police chief, he was concerned about everyone who served under him, but his friends took a little bit more from him when they were injured.

"He was shot, the shot creasing the side of his head. He's suffering from headaches. Unfortunately, he can't remember the last twenty-four to forty-eight hours."

"And he should is what you are not saying. Where is my son?" Ardeen headed for the door, Alin on her heels.

Toryn watched them walk into the house, turning once more to the road as he heard footsteps. Lyle approached him as did Aaron, the deputy chief.

"How is Aidan?" Lyle went right to the point.

"He's fighting us on staying quiet. I pray that Artis is able to convince him to take it easy. I can't guarantee that she will win. He's too stubborn at times."

"He is." Aaron spoke up. He knew the character of Aidan and that he would not stop until he solved his own mystery.

"We're not going to be able to stop him." Lyle frowned as he saw two men standing across the street watching them. "Do you know those men?"

—

The two with him turned to study the men, shaking their heads. They shared a look but when they looked back, the men had disappeared.

"Where did they go?" Lyle was across the street, Toryn following, to search for them. "They were here. I saw them."

"We all saw them." Toryn grew quiet, a thought crossing his mind that God had provided help for Aidan and Artis. Were these the men? And were they just men or angels in disguise?

Chapter 8

Ardeen paused as she approached the entrance to the living room. She recognized her son's voice and that of Slaney. She didn't recognize the other lady's. Alin's hand rested on her shoulder as he stood tried to place the voice but couldn't. He moved past Ardeen to stare at the three in the room. A frown covered his face.

Aidan looked up suddenly, sensing others in the room. He rose to his feet, leaving Artis staring up at him.

"Dad? You're here." He reached to hug his father and then his mother. "Mom? How was the flight?"

"It was fine and uneventful. Son, introduce us to this lady."

Aidan drew in a deep breath. This is it, he thought. His hand reached for Artis, drawing her to her feet and to his side.

"Mom, Dad. This is Artis. She's my bride." Aidan had his eyes on Artis and missed the looks on his parent's faces.

"Your bride? I don't understand." Ardeen moved in on her son to hug him once more before she turned to face Artis. "And this lovely lady is she?" Ardeen simply reached to hug her, taking in the lost and frightened at the same time.

———

"This is Artis, Mom." Aidan repeated himself without realizing it. "We married yesterday. She's in danger."

"And you stepped in, son." Alin moved in on Artis, nudging Ardeen aside. He too hugged Artis before he stepped back to drape an arm across his son's shoulder.

"I did, Dad. She didn't have anyone else." Aidan sounded almost desperate for his parents to understand.

"We understand, son. We truly do." Ardeen had an arm around Artis. "What can we do for you two?"

Artis shrugged, not sure of what was happening. Her eyes were on Aidan, seeing that he would be there for her. She sighed. This was not how she had planned the next few days.

Aidan moved to wrap Artis in his arms, his prayer whispering in her ear. He held on for a bit longer before he turned to face the others in the room. He nodded at Lyle and Aaron, knowing that Toryn would have asked for them to be there.

"Can we sit?" Artis almost shoved Aidan into his chair and reclaimed the ottoman beside him, feeling his arm around her.

"We can do that, Artis." Ardeen sat close to her son, wanting to take the burden from him but knowing that this was something that he was bearing himself. All they could do was support him.

Slaney approached them with trays in her hands, Toryn and Lyle following her with trays of their own.

—

The food as dispersed among the group before Alin led them in a prayer over their food. He kept an eye on his son and his bride, not quite sure how to approach them.

"Can we spend some time in prayer, Dad?" Aidan looked up to see Gideon had joined them. He nodded at his friend, knowing that Gideon would offer what counsel that he could.

The time of prayer finished, Aidan stared at Artis. He could not remember what had happened and would need to depend on her recollection to describe what had happened.

"Artis?" Toryn waited for her to look at him. "Can you explain to us what happened? I know that you did give a statement yesterday. Sometimes, going back over it will allow you to remember something."

Artis nodded, knowing that was only too true. She had seen it with her own work. She turned to Aidan to find him focused on her.

"Okay. So where do I start?" Artis was struggling at the moment, fatigue hitting hard. She blinked for a moment before her eyes closed and she slept. Toryn was on his feet to catch her as she slid from the ottoman, looking around at Aidan. Artis roused quickly, apologizing for sleeping and reclaimed her seat. Aidan had given her a nod, wanting to hear what she had to say, seeing that he could not remember anything.

"Start with your work, Artis. Help us to understand what you do for work. That may lead to understanding why you were kidnapped." Toryn nodded at her in a compassionate manner. "It's okay.

Everyone can stay. It will help us understand who you are and why this might have happened to you."

Artis had focused her eyes on Toryn as he spoke. She knew that he was speaking the truth.

"All right. My occupation is a youth protective worker. I had just quit my job and decided that I needed to take some time to figure out what I wanted to do. You can understand the burn-out rate with that work. I had rented a cabin just for a week or so just to get away from everything. That was close to where Aidan had rented his. I was at the diner for a meal, walking over to it. Aidan was there and as we finished he joined me and then was walking with me to his truck. He refused to let me walk back to my cabin. He rushed away from the diner and that's when we were stopped in the parking lot and taken captive.

"The men finally stopped the truck and made us walk to the cave. Aidan stood in front of me to protect me. I'm not sure why he was shot but it was deliberate. I think Aidan moved his head to the side to avoid the bullet. I really think that they meant to kill him. They refused to get me anything to take care of him. Instead, the entrance was blocked with branches. I heard them outside of it over the day.

"The next morning, I woke up in a cabin. I don't remember moving there. Gabe and Mike took care of us, made sure that Aidan was looked at in a hospital, and then headed this way. Gabe insisted that we marry, stating that it might be the only way that I could stay safe. I just worry that they'll go after Aidan just to get to me."

"They might, Artis." Lyle shared a look with George. "Can you describe Gabe and Mike?"

"I can. Gabe was older, in his forties, I think. He had blond hair, a darker blond beard, and blue eyes. Mike was younger, around our age. He also had blond hair and blue eyes. I don't know if they were related or not. But they did look familiar." Artis looked around at Aidan, seeing the pain that he was trying hard to hide. "Aidan? Do you remember anything?"

"No, Artis, I don't. I wish that I did. I remember getting up that morning but nothing past around nine o'clock. The physician this morning said that it was not unusual. He felt that I might remember in time."

"I pray that you do. Someone needs to confirm this and that I didn't trap you into marriage." She was sober as she said that.

"None of us think that, Artis. We have had friends go through some pretty dangerous stuff. So, we want to work with you and Aidan to discover who this is." Lyle nodded towards Aidan. "He'll be investigating it as soon as he can."

They all watched as Artis turned to study Aidan who was studying her in turn. They could feel the attraction between the two. It just worried them all that the two were in danger and they didn't know who from.

—

Chapter 9

The next morning, Aidan was on his feet early in the morning. He paused outside the bedroom which Artis had chosen before he moved onto the kitchen. Squinting at the clock, he sighed. It was too early for anyone to be up but he had risen at this time of day for years. It was a hard habit to break.

Walking back to his office, his mug of coffee landed on his desk before he sat in the chair and pulled it forward. His elbows on his desk, he cradled his head. This was not how his vacation was to go. Not one bit. But he also acknowledged that God was in control and that He had a plan and purpose for his life that he didn't understand. All he knew was that he had a lady in his life who he needed to protect. Only he had no idea how he would do that when he was injured. Aidan also had no idea who he was protecting her from.

Aidan reached for his Bible, needing the peace that only God could bring. He knew from the experiences that he had been through while working with his friends just how much that was needed.

Artis was on her feet two hours later, wondering that she had even been able to sleep. She felt somewhat refreshed but still very worried about Aidan. He had been hurt because of her. That injury would prevent him from returning to work soon. That distressed her.

Looking for Aidan, Artis wandered through the house that now seemed to be her home. She sighed. She had given up her apartment, placed everything but what she really needed into storage, and headed out the week before. An email had been sent to her parents. She had heard back from her father, just stating that they were praying for her. He trusted her judgement in what she was doing but asked that she keep them informed of where she was. Artis had no idea how to do that. Aidan had provided the wireless internet connection that she needed.

She reached for her laptop and pulled up her email. Breathing a sigh of relief, she read the emails from her parents. Artis knew that she had no option but to confess what had happened to her. She just didn't know if she was ready to.

Aidan paused in the hallway, watching Artis as she sat at the kitchen table. He was at a loss as to what to do or say. This was all new territory for him. He could understand now to a certain extent what his friends had gone through.

A hand rested on Artis' shoulder, bringing her back to the kitchen. She looked up, a frown on her face. Aidan's face had bruised and she could see the pain in his eyes. That worried her.

"Aidan? Should you be up?" Aidan's hand kept her in her chair.

"I need to be, Artis. I'll rest later. You were lost in thought." He pulled out a chair to sit beside her, his head tilted as he studied the sober look on her face.

"I was. I was composing an email to Mom and Dad. How do I tell them something like this when they are so far away? They know that I quit my job, closed my apartment, and had set off for a vacation." She snorted, causing Aidan to grin. "This really is not the vacation that I planned. Nor was it yours."

"No, it wasn't. But I fully understand that it was God's plan for us." Aidan grew silent for a moment. "I'm sorry that it had to be like this, Artis. I truly am. You should have been wooed and courted and been able to enjoy the dating aspect."

Artis nodded. She had had to give that to God but she knew that somehow this was God's plan. She just had to understand that she couldn't understand the bigger picture that was that plan.

"It's okay, Aidan. How are you feeling? And don't tell me fine because I know that you're not." Artis glared at him as he grinned at her.

"I won't then. The headache is there, not quite as bad but still enough that I don't know how much I can do today." Aidan sighed. "This is not how this should be, Artis."

"I know, Aidan. How well I know that!" Artis dropped her head into her hands, a deep shudder running through her body. "We need to investigate this, Aidan. I know that's what you do. How do we proceed?"

"We don't have much information as yet. I think that you were the target. I was incidental to that, just being there in the way as it could be said. We need to look back over who you helped and who might have threatened you. How do we do that since you resigned?"

—

"I sent in an email to my former boss, letting him know what happened. He is willing to work as much as he can. He stated that whoever the investigator is here should contact him and then he'd have to look at search warrants for that information."

Aidan nodded. It was about how he expected it to be.

"I have a friend who could look into it for us. She finds people and information that no one else seems to be able to. If you want, I'll send it on to her."

"We need to do something, Aidan. We need to resolve this as soon as we can. If that is even possible." Artis hesitated for a moment before she looked up at him again. She frowned at the look in his eyes. She wasn't sure what to think. "Aidan, where do we go from here?"

"I don't know, Artis. I really don't. I need to heal. You need to heal as well. You're burnt out from your work. I also suspect that you are running from someone."

Artis stared at him, her eyes huge. Aidan had just pinpointed what she felt.

"That's it, Aidan. I am running and I don't know from whom or why." Artis buried her face in her hands and then jumped as she felt Aidan's arms around her. His prayer whispered in her ears, a prayer that was laced with Bible verses and God's promises. She sensed his promise to her as well that he would do everything that he could to protect her.

Aidan raised his head at last, studying the beautiful lady who was his bride. He was close enough to see the faint sprinkling of freckles on her face, which only endeared her to him even more.

"Can you share with me who you think it is? I know with your work that you might not be able to."

Artis nodded, her heart heavy with her thoughts and the danger that they were in. A chime from her phone had her reaching for it. A frown and then a smile crossed her face.

"Mom and Dad are heading home. They'll be here tomorrow." Artis then frowned at Aidan. "How do we explain us to them?"

Chapter 10

The next afternoon, Artis paced the house. Her parents were on their way there, surprised at the address and the town. She could hear the questions that they were not asking and really wasn't sure how she would respond when she saw them. Aidan leaned against a door frame and watched her, his heart praying for his lady. He had begun to think of her as that and had no desire to look into a future that didn't include her. She challenged him almost hourly with her questions and her responses to his questions. His father had laughed at him that morning, simply stating that it served him right and that it was about time that someone stopped him in his tracks. Ardeen had laughed as well as she hugged Artis, turning the younger lady to the outdoors and a seat in the yard. She had simply prayed for her daughter-in-law.

The sudden ringing of the doorbell startled Artis and she spun to stare that way. Aidan hugged her on the way by before he opened the door. He frowned for a moment before his face cleared. Artis looked like her mother.

"You must be Artis' parents. Come in. I'm Aidan McNeill." Aidan reached to shake their hands. "Artis is in the living room." He hesitated for a moment as he saw them exchanging glances.

"We don't understand." Bayne Aislinn hesitated for a moment. He had noted the wedding band on Aidan's hand. He couldn't understand what Artis was doing there.

"Come on in. Artis is waiting for you." Aidan pointed towards the living, watching as Bayne and Bridy moved towards there. He heard the sob that Artis gave before she was in her mother's arms, unable to control her tears.

Bayne reached for his daughter at last, a father's prayer whispered in her ear. He stood back and watched her, seeing her hesitancy that was so unlike her.

"Artis? What's going on? We weren't expecting to find you here." Bridy hesitated before she reached for Artis' hand. "Artis? What is this? You haven't been dating anyone."

Artis' eyes rose to Aidan before she broke away from her mother and almost threw herself at Aidan. His arms closed around her for a moment, his head down on hers even though the force with which she hit his body caused his head to pound.

Bayne and Bridy shared a look, a puzzled and worried look at that. This was not Artis to do this. Something had happened that had changed her to this.

"Artis? Can you explain?" Bayne finally broke the silence that hang heavy in the air.

Artis nodded, not willing to speak. Aidan looked around his living room, taking in the soft autumn colours that he had chosen. He nodded towards the couch.

"Artis, have a seat with your mom. I'll be back in just a moment." He walked away and returned with a tray of coffee and tea in mugs. Artis had told him that her parents preferred tea and he was happy to oblige them.

"Mr. and Mrs. Aislinn, we do need to explain what happened. But I think that we need to spend time in prayer first." Aidan looked down, not wanting to see censure on their faces.

"We can do that, son. You're bearing a heavy burden, I can tell. Not to mention that you have been injured in some way." Bayne simply bowed his head and prayed for his daughter and the young man whose side she didn't seem to want to leave.

Bayne looked up at last, peace in his heart about his daughter. Something had happened, that much he knew, and that was why he and Bridy had returned home so quickly.

"Artis? Talk to us. Tell us what has happened. We know that you resigned from your work, stored your furniture, and was planning to take a vacation until you decided what you wanted to do."

"That was my plan, Dad." Artis started at the floor, not willing to look up at her father. "God had other plans." Her words stopped as she was unable to continue. She felt Aidan's arm around her.

"I guess it's up to me. I am a police detective. I am not sure how that will play out in our adventure. On Friday, I was in a diner while on vacation and found Artis there. I sensed danger around her and tried to get her to safety. That didn't happen. We were kidnapped. While we were enclosed in a cave, one of the kidnappers shot me." Aidan pointed to the bandage on the side of his head. "I am recovering, thank God.

———

Some men rescued us from what Artis tells me. She also tells me that one of them suggested that we marry so that Artis would have my protection but also the protection of the force here. So we did. We have no idea who was behind the kidnapping or why it happened. My friends on the force are working on this. I will be as well." Aidan looked up at that point, not finding anything but sympathy, compassion and trust on the older couple's faces.

"I see." Bayne sat back in his chair, his hands folded on his abdomen. Artis recognized that as her father's position when he was deep in thought. "Thank you for stepping in, Aidan, if I may call you that. You are family now."

"Thank you. You have my pledge that I will do my best to protect Artis." Aidan studied Artis, finding her studying her parents. "Artis?"

"Dad's right. You are family now. We need to work this through." Artis sighed. "I have no idea what is going on, Mom, Dad. No one does at this point. However, we will start working on it. Dad? What contact do you have that we can reach out to?" Bayne was a retired officer who still had many contacts that he would be contacting.

"I have some that I'll reach out to. For now, what can we do for you?" Bayne shared a look with Bridy. "We're close enough to here that we can come back and forth as we need to."

Aidan nodded, knowing that Bayne was being careful not to cross any boundaries. He appreciated that.

—

"Thank you. Now, we need to make some plans. Artis will want her things here to make her feel at home." Aidan rubbed at his temple, the headache worsening from stress.

"We can do that, son. But for now, what do we do?" Bridy moved to sit beside her daughter, wrapping an arm around her. "Artis? What are your thoughts?"

"My thoughts?" Artis gave a harsh laugh that contained sobs. "I don't have any thoughts, Mom. I just don't." She buried her head on her mother's shoulders, just needing her mother.

Chapter 11

Bayne was on his feet, walking away from his ladies. He was distraught at what Artis had told him. It was not what he had been expecting to hear, not at all. He turned to watch them before Aidan's hand on his shoulder turned him to the kitchen.

Aidan had an eye on the clock. He didn't think any of them really felt like eating but he was determined to do something for a meal and to find something that Bayne could help with.

"Aidan? Did that really happen?"

"It did, Mr. Aislinn." Aidan stopped as Bayne shook his head.

"Call us Bayne and Bridy. You're family now." Bayne leaned against the counter, his eyes on the doorway. "I don't understand why Artis."

"We don't either. Artis thinks it is related to a previous client. We haven't been able to confirm anything as yet. It's too soon for that. What we have to do is keep her safe. And I don't think that is going to be easy."

Bayne snorted, knowing his daughter only too well. She would not stay hidden. She would be out there looking for whoever it was. And that could mean harm or death for his daughter.

"I don't think she'll sit back and not be out there looking for the men." Bayne studied the younger man, seeing the strength of his character. Bayne had learned early how to read people. He liked what he saw in Aidan.

"I know that she will. And she can't." Aidan sighed. "And I will be out there with her. I can investigate but I have to turn everything over to someone else to have it verified." Aidan looked around as he heard the doorbell. He sighed. He wanted to continue his conversation with Bayne and see if he had any idea of who it was. That would have to wait.

Alin and Ardeen stepped into the house, pausing for a moment as they heard voices. Ardeen hugged her son, a question on her face.

"Aidan. You have company. I'm sorry that we didn't know that." Alin laid a hand on his son's shoulder.

"It's okay, Dad. You need to meet them. Artis' parents, Bayne and Bridy, are here."

"I know a Bayne Aislinn." Alin headed for where he could hear movement in the kitchen. "Bayne?"

Bayne spun as he heard Alin, surprise on his face.

"Alin? You're Aidan's father? I didn't know that."

"I am. It's good to see you again, even under the circumstances. We can use your expertise in this." Alin turned as he heard footsteps behind him. "Bridy? It's good to see you again."

"It is, Alin. I didn't expect us to become related like this." Bridy hugged him and then turned to Ardeen. "Ardeen?" She stood back watching the other lady.

"It's been a shock, I must say, Bridy." Bayne's arm was around his wife, worried about her. She had decided to retire due to health issues and the trip that they had just returned to had been cut short not just because of Artis' danger.

Aidan searched for Artis, finding her in the sunroom, standing and staring out of the window. His arms came around her.

"Okay, darling?" His voice was kept low as he struggled with his own emotions.

Artis shook her head. She was not okay, she decided. Her emotions were all over the place. Artis had pried into her mother's return early from her trip and was dismayed to hear that her mother was not well and that was why they had returned early.

"Mom's sick. She hasn't said what but I'm scared for her." She felt Aidan's arms tighten around her. "And now this, whatever it is that we are involved in. This is not how we need to be living."

"I know, sweetheart. What can I do for you?"

Artis struggled in Aidan's arms until she could face him. She searched his face, seeing his concern for her in his eyes.

"You're in pain, Aidan. You need to rest." She shoved at him until he stepped back. "Please, Aidan? Please sit."

Aidan nodded and reached for her hand, drawing her down to the couch with him. His finger rubbed at her wedding band that matched his.

"I'm sorry that we married as we did. I'm not sorry that it's you." He reached into his pocket, drawing out a small box. "Would you wear this?"

Artis stared at the beautiful emerald ring that he held out for her. She looked up at him, seeing his patience in waiting for her to reply. She nodded and then watched as he slid the ring onto her finger. He didn't tell her the history of it. That would come at a later day.

Aidan waited for a reaction from Artis. He didn't have to wait long. She reached to hug him before she sat back, her eyes on the ring.

"There's a story here, Aidan." She looked up at him before she looked around the sunroom, taking in the plants that he had placed at strategic places in the room. She liked the brown wicker furniture, the soft green walls, and the few photographs that he had enlarged, framed, and hung on the wall.

"There is, Artis. It was a grandmother's ring. She was from Ireland and my grandfather gave it to her as a reminder of the Emerald Island."

"That is so sweet. And they gave it to you." Artis studied Aidan, seeing the response on his face.

"They did. There is more to the story. I'll share it with you at some point." Aidan lifted her hand and kissed the back of it, surprising both of them.

—

Chapter 12

Bridy came searching for her daughter, hesitating to disturb the couple. Artis was on her feet, moving towards her mother, a questioning look on her face.

"Mom? You wanted something?" Artis reached to hug her mother again.

"Not really, love. I just wanted to make sure that you were all right." Bridy turned Artis back to face Aidan. "We're not staying here. Dad has found a place for us for now." Bridy studied her daughter. "Are you sure?"

Artis knew what her mother was asking without putting it into words. She was asking if her daughter was okay with being married as she had been and then what her parents could do for her.

"I'm fine, Mom. We'll talk at some point. For now, it's okay." Artis felt Aidan's arm around her and leaned against him. "Don't do God's work for Him, Mom. I know that you worry and it's right that you do. But God is here and in control. He has a purpose and plan for us that we don't see or understand at the moment. He will use us to bring someone to justice. We have to trust Him no matter how hard that is." Artis could feel Aidan nodding against her head and knew that he agreed with her.

"Artis is right. God is in control. It doesn't mean that we won't go through difficulties or danger or harm but He wants only the best for us." Aidan bit at his lip for a moment, not quite sure how to word what he needed to say. "I know that I am a police officer. That doesn't mean that I won't go through difficulties and danger in my personal life. I have seen it happen to friends."

Bridy was watching him closely, seeing the distress that he was feeling.

"I see. We'll talk about that at some point, Aidan. For now, what can we do for you?"

Artis turned to Aidan, finding him watching her. She could see the pain on his face and turned him towards the hallway before shoving him towards his bedroom.

"You need to rest, Aidan. Our parents will stay for a while. But please? Lie down."

Aidan nodded. His head was pounding and he did need to rest. He just didn't want to. He curled up under a blanket, his eyes closing as he slept. He felt Artis' light kiss on his cheek in his dreams and a smile crossed his face.

Artis quietly closed the door behind her, leaving Aidan sleeping. She tilted her head before she nodded. George was here. She prayed that he would have the answers that would solve whatever it was that they were involved in. However, Artis knew that would not likely be the case.

George turned as he felt a touch on his arm. Artis had found him.

"George? Do you need to speak with Aidan? I just got him to lie down. His head is aching but he wouldn't tell anyone."

"No, he wouldn't. He's like that. He puts others ahead of himself." George grinned at Artis. "How are you, Artis?"

Artis shrugged. She was not sure how to answer that question.

"I'm not sure how to respond, George. I want this over. Can you do that?" Artis glared at George as his grin widened.

"I am sure that you do want this over. We want it over for you as well. Now, where can we talk?" George followed Artis to the office and dropped the folders that he was holding onto the table.

"What do you have to tell us, George?" Artis found a seat on the couch and wrapped her arms around a pillow. She was not sure what he would tell her and she needed to remember it to explain it to Aidan.

"I'll go over what I have with you and then leave the information with you for Aidan." George looked down at the floor and took the time to gather his thoughts. He looked up at Artis, finding her watching him with a calm look on her face. He knew that she was afraid but given the line of work that she was in, she had learned to hide her emotions. George knew that Aidan did the same as did he and any other officer that he knew.

"Thank you, George. Go ahead. Tell me what you need to."

"Right to the point? I like that." George reached for the folders and handed them to Artis. "This is what we have. We don't have a lot of information right now, unfortunately. Aidan will want to see what we have. I know that he will."

"Of course, he will. I would expect nothing less than that." Artis looked towards the doorway, expecting Aidan to appear. Only he didn't. "So, George, how do we do this?"

"I am not sure at this point, Artis. We don't have a lot of information on the men who abducted you. I know that you worked with a sketch artist and we have them out to see if anyone recognizes them. So far, we have not had a positive response on that." George was at a loss to explain what had happened to Aidan and Artis.

"I didn't expect that anyone would. It is just so bizarre."

"It is, Artis. We can't get a handle on who or why. Have you thought any more about that?" George was frustrated.

"You're frustrated, George." Artis looked at him with sympathy on her face. "You need Aidan to work with you and he can't. Not right at the moment. What can we do for you?" Artis was reaching out to him in a way that only she could.

"I do, Artis. Not many people understand how we work. We work as a team. When one of our team is down, it affects all of us." George blew out a big breath. "Thank you for understanding."

Artis shrugged. It really wasn't that hard to understand what George needed. He needed the man who had helped to train him and who was a sounding board for him. AndAidan was not available.

"I understand that, George." Artis pointed at the folders. "Now, talk to me. Tell me what you can."

Chapter 13

On his feet a number of hours later, Aidan searched for Artis. He found her curled up on her bed and asleep with traces of tears on her face. He dropped to his knees beside the bed, his arms around her, his head buried against hers. All he could do was pray for his lady and what they were going through.

Aidan walked through to his office, frowning at the file folders neatly stacked on his desk. He opened one and then dropped into his chair, reading through the material. His thoughts were the same as George's. They really had no idea who had been after Artis and if they still were. There was also no clear reason why. That frightened him and not much frightened the seasoned police officer.

He looked around as he heard the doorbell and was on his feet to open the door. Lyle and Toryn stood there, grim looks on their faces. This can't be good, he knew, for them to show up and look as they did.

"Guys? You're here. I don't like the looks on your faces." Aidan pointed to the kitchen. "I'm just about to start some coffee." He squinted at the clock. It was suppertime but he really didn't feel like eating.

"Sit, Aidan. You're still really rocky on your feet." Lyle moved past him to set the coffee. "Where's your wife?"

"She's sleeping. It looks as if George was around when I was sleeping."

—

“He was.” Lyle confirmed that. “He said that he spoke with Artis and then left some folders of information for you.”

“I found them. I just don’t understand where’s he heading with his thoughts.”

“He’s not sure either. He wants to speak with you but is off for the next couple of days.” Toryn reached for his mug of coffee, setting Aidan’s mug in front of him. “Let’s pray, Aidan. This is not going to be solved tomorrow. And we fear for you and Artis. Unfortunately, we know only too well what we are looking at. That doesn’t make it any easier for you.”

“No, it doesn’t. I can’t explain what happened. Artis and I have spoken about this. She didn’t recognize the men. I can’t remember them enough to know if I do or not. George left the sketches for me to look at. They’re strangers to me.” Aidan shifted on his chair before he rubbed at his forehead. His head was aching again. He just wanted it to stop hurting. Aidan also wanted to go on with his life with Artis. He just didn’t know if Artis would stay with him. “Have you found out anything about the two men who helped us?”

“No, we haven’t. That’s not unusual you know. That does happen sometimes.” Toryn frowned at Aidan before he shared a look with Lyle. “What are your thoughts, Aidan?”

“Artis is convinced that they are angels, sent to protect us. I have to say that’s the way I’m thinking.” Aidan looked at the two men with him. “It’s happened before with people. Angels have stepped in to help.”

—

69

"We know, Aidan. It's entirely possible that they were or are angels. Your neighbours have reported men matching their description around here but when they approach them, the men have disappeared."

Aidan turned as he heard a sudden noise outside and was on his feet. A hand on his arm stopped him in his tracks as Toryn moved past him and halted Aidan's steps. Toryn headed out of the back door as Lyle headed out of the front door. The men searched, not finding what caused the commotion before they stood on the sidewalk near the road.

"What was that, Toryn?" Lyle studied the surrounding area. "It was something that we all heard."

"It was." Toryn walked back around the house, pausing near the front porch. He beckoned to Lyle. "This. This is what we hear." He pointed at a box that had been tucked down into a shrub. "We'll need a team to come through."

Lyle nodded as he reached for his phone. This was what they had been expecting but praying would not happen. He looked up to see Aidan on the porch, his arm around Artis. Artis looked a little bewildered before she yawned and leaned her head against Aidan. A grim smile crossed his face.

Toryn walked towards him, a crime scene tech beside him. Lyle turned away from the porch, a questioning look on his face.

"Whoever it is? They're staying close to Aidan and Artis. That's what we figured out that they were doing." Toryn was frustrated. He knew only too well how it felt to be on that end of the investigation. "What do we really know, Lyle?"

Lyle shrugged, reaching for the evidence bags. He studied the contents, a sigh rising within him.

"These photos show that they are close to these two. And we can't be with them all the time. They would allow us even if we could. Aidan needs to heal. He'll want back to work soon."

"He will." Toryn took the evidence bags, his eyes on Aidan and Artis as they approached. "We have to tell them, Lyle. This is not something that we can keep from them."

"No, it's not." He turned as he heard the footsteps behind him. Of course, they would be there.

Aidan reached for the bags, reading the letters, Artis leaning against him as he did so. The letters were vague, just warning the couple that they were being watched and that they would not be safe anywhere. It was only a matter of time, the last letter said.

"They're doing this?" Artis was not surprised. In fact, she had expected this.

"They are, Artis. Do you have any idea who would be doing this?" Lyle's voice was stern as was his face. He watched as she shook her head.

"I don't, Lyle. I really don't. If I had any idea, I would be all over them. I want this over." Artis turned and stalked back to the house, not letting the men see the tears sparkling on her cheeks.

"And she would do that, Lyle. She's not one to sit back and wait." Aidan walked after Artis, reaching

—

to wrap her in his arms. He held her as she struggled to control her emotions, a prayer whispering in her ears.

Chapter 14

A week later, Artis wandered the downtown area of Oak City. She had needed to get away from the house. Aidan was working on their adventure, as he called it, along with a friend of his named Don. Don had arrived not that long ago, stating that he was here to help. Artis had looked at him, a frown on her face as he grinned at her and then told her that he had a security team. And yes, his team had gone through similar adventures.

Aidan had watched as Artis' face had shuttered before she walked away. He was worried about her. She was not talking to him and they needed her to do that.

Turning to enter a shop, Artis hesitated. She saw a man watching her before he walked towards her.

"Gabe? What do you want?" Artis scowled at him.

Gabe smiled at her, a hand out to stop her from backing away from him.

"I just wanted to see how you two are. We're watching out for you, Artis."

"Are you? I don't see that you are." Artis refused to back down from Gabe. "Where's Mike?"

"He's watching your house. He won't be found, though, Artis. We have taken steps to stay hidden."

Artis looked into the shop window for a few seconds and then back at Gabe. Only Gabe was no longer standing in front of her. She spun to search for him before she stopped. God had sent Gabe once more. She wondered what God had prevented from happening to her.

Aidan looked up at last, hearing Artis moving around the house. He was on his feet, heading her way. He watched her for a moment before he wrapped her in a hug. Artis hugged him back, needing that contact with him.

"Artis? What happened? I know that something did." Aidan leaned back to look down at her face.

"Have you seen Gabe and Mike around here?" Artis stared up at Aidan, amazed once more at his height.

"No, I haven't. I didn't expect to. Why do you ask?"

"Because Gabe found me this morning. He said that Mike was around here, watching out for you."

"He is? I haven't seen him. There's more." Aidan waited patiently for Artis to gather her thoughts.

"Gabe was talking to me. I looked in a store window and when I looked back, Gabe was gone. There was nothing to show that he was ever there. Are they angels?"

"They may be, Artis. I can't explain how they just disappear like that." Aidan hugged her tighter. There was no real explanation for how the two men were disappearing as they were.

—

"What did you find out?" Artis changed the subject, knowing that Aidan had been working away on what he had available

"Not a lot, Artis." Aidan stepped back, his eyes on the floor. "I think that we need to take a trip to your home town and bring your things here."

Artis had turned away from him and spun back, surprise on her face. He was speaking as if she would live there the rest of her life. She had not been expecting that.

"Aidan? What are you saying?"

Aidan did not look at her. He didn't want to see the rejection on her face that he thought would be there.

"I don't want you to leave, Artis. I love you, as quickly as this has been. You are who I have been waiting for. You are the missing part of my heart. That's what the emerald ring means." He stood, shoulders braced for her rejection.

Artis stared at him, shock and then wonder on her face. He loved her? It was too soon, wasn't it? Then she moved towards him, a hand out to touch his cheek and turn him towards her. God did work in ways that they didn't understand.

"Aidan? Do you mean that?" Artis kept her hand on his cheek.

Aidan nodded. He knew that it seemed to be too soon but he knew others that had fallen in love as quickly as he had. He searched her face, stopping as he read the answer in her eyes.

—

"Artis?"

"I love you too, Aidan. I just thought that it was too soon."

Aidan's kiss stopped her words. He then just held her.

Don Devlin, a friend of Aidan's, turned back to face the front door as Aidan opened it. He stepped inside, a quizzical look on his face. Aidan had reached out to him and asked him to stop by. He had something that he needed to ask him and he was Artis to be part of the discussion.

"Aidan? What's going on?" Don looked past him at Artis as she stood, shifting from foot to foot. "Artis?"

"Don, come on into the office. We need to make some plans and we're thinking that we need your team's help. Your ladies as well." Aidan reached for Artis' hand as they sat, Don finding a seat near them.

"Can we pray first?" Artis was hesitant to ask.

"That's what I was going to suggest, Artis. You two are in the middle of something that no one can see the end to. I can understand to a certain extent what you are going through. What was it that you wanted to ask?"

"Artis has her belongings in her home town. We want to go there this weekend and retrieve them. She'll bring her personal things here and we'll put everything else into storage until we decide what to keep or not keep." Aidan's hand tightened on Artis' hand.

“I see. And you want my team to come along?” Don had a security team and all of them had been through danger with their ladies.

“We do. The ladies as well if possible. Artis needs to know that she is not alone.” Aidan eyed Artis, finding her watching Don. “Artis?”

“It’s okay.” She frowned at Don. “I know you.”

Don nodded. She did in fact know him.

“You do. My team provided security for that teen and his mother.” Don didn’t say much more than that, but Aidan was quick to see that Artis had relaxed as Don acknowledged that. “And I have been around with other teams at time, Artis.”

“And all I can do is thank you and your team, Don. There were some dangerous times when you stepped in. Now, when do we go to my home town?”

“Saturday, I think. It’s what about two hours away?”

Artis nodded. This step would cut her ties with her home town but it was only right. God was leading in this and all she could do was follow the path that He was laying out for her.

Chapter 15

Saturday found Artis staring at the storage unit that held her belongings. She knew that Don and his team were behind her as were their ladies. Aidan had his arm around her even as he prayed for her and their time there that morning. Artis had come to realize that Aidan did very little without praying about it first. He told her that was what had kept him safe many times over the years. He had developed a sense of when to move forward and when to wait. He was in that close of a walk with God.

"Are you ready to do this, sweetheart?" Aidan spoke at last, shifting to stare behind him at Don, shrugging as he did so.

"I guess." Artis sighed. She could feel someone watching her and that person was evil. She had the ability to sense that about people. She had hated it as a teenager but had been grateful for that in her working life. "We're sure about this"

"We are. We've talked it over and prayed it through." Aidan reached for the key and unlocked the padlock that had shut the locker tight.

Don reached to roll up the door, Paul and Thomas standing on either side of the couple. Mark, Joshua, and Caleb stood with their backs to the couple, watching the area around them. They could sense danger approaching and were willing to put their lives on the line to protect their friends. They had gone into work mode. Their wives looked at their husbands and then at one another before they too shrugged.

—

The many hands that were there made light work of loading the rental truck that Don had provided for them. Artis was sober as they finished before she walked to the office for the storage facility. Mark and Joshua walked with her despite the frowns that she kept sending their way. They just grinned at her and kept walking. They could still feel the danger around her and Aidan. There was no way that they were letting her walk around on her own.

Artis stood for a moment on the pavement just outside of the office. *This was it,* she decided. *This is when and how I leave my hometown. I'm not that far from here but I don't know that I'll come back here much. Mom and Dad are retired now and are looking to leave here as well. What do we do, Lord? How do we go forward with the plans and purposes that You have for our lives? I don't see what You are planning but I know that You have only the best in mind for us. I just fear what we need to go through to get to that.*

Mark looked around before he turned in a complete circle. Someone was out there, very close to them. His hand went out to grasp Artis' arm, startling her.

"Come on, Artis. We need to get out of here." He almost ran towards the storage unit where everyone was still gathered.

Joshua hesitated a moment, scanning the area around them before he too ran towards the group. The two men could hear a commotion behind them and picked up their pace. The others spun to stare at them before they scattered to the vehicles, sorting themselves out. Don shoved Aidan and Artis into his truck before driving away in the centre of the convoy of vehicles. Aidan stared behind him, seeimg the three men who had appeared. He could see the weapons in their hand. Artis was staring back as well, shock on her face.

"It was that close, Aidan?" She was unable to believe that they had just escaped the men.

"It was, sweetheart. It was." He reached for her hand, his grip tight on it. "Don?"

"I'll need to talk to Mark and Joshua. Something triggered with them for them to run towards us like that. Artis? Did you see anyone?" Don shot a glance over his shoulder towards her.

"No, I didn't. I didn't feel comfortable but I thought it was just my emotions. Guess it wasn't." Artis grew quiet, fear coursing through her. She didn't want to be in this position of fear and worry but she was.

Aidan walked through their home later that afternoon. They had brought in the boxes that Artis stated that she wanted there but placed the other boxes and furniture into a storage unit that was owned by a fellow officer. That gave them both a certain sense of safety. Aidan was still worried about Artis. He had been to the police physician the day before and was cleared to go back to desk work on a part-time basis. He was deeply worried about leaving Artis on her own.

Artis turned from where she had been placing books on the book shelves in the office. She really didn't have that many that she wanted to keep. That surprised her. She loved reading and had been adamant that she would not give up any books

His arms wrapping her in a hug, Aidan kissed her and then just stood, holding the love of his life in his arms. She leaned against him, content to be held but knowing that they did need to talk about what had happened earlier that day.

"We'll talk, sweetheart. We'll talk." Aidan turned her towards the kitchen. "I have a light meal ready for us. I know. We don't feel like eating after what happened earlier." He seated her and then sat himself, their meal in front of them.

Artis sighed at last, showing away the plate. She had tried to eat but that hadn't been easy to do. She had no appetite to finish the meal. Artis knew that Aidan had been having the same difficulty as she had.

Aidan cleared away the remnants of their meal, his hand on Artis' shoulder keeping her in her chair. He sat beside her, wrapping her in his arms and bent his head to pray for them. Artis followed his lead with her own petitions, not sure that they were being heard despite God's promises that they were.

"What happened today, Aidan?" Artis broke the silence in the room.

"We were likely followed. And I would suspect that you were followed when you put your stuff there. It's not really that secure even though there is fencing around it." Aidan could only offer a prayer of thanks that nothing had happened to her when she had done that. "You had friends help you move your things?"

—

Artis nodded, a thoughtful look on her face.

"I did." She sighed. "Has George looked into them?"

"I am not sure that he has. Let me have a list and I'll send it on to him. I also have a friend, a lady named Emma, who has a business tracking people. I have spoken to her briefly. We can send on everything we have to her and she'll work it. She finds information and people that no one else can." Aidan tilted his head to watch Artis. He frowned at the contented look on her face. "Artis?"

"It's okay, Aidan. I know Emma and her husband and his team. We've worked together in the past." She snuggled closer to him. "It's Sunday tomorrow."

"It is. Gideon was around when you were busy in the office. He just wanted to let me know that the officers who attend there have taken precautions to keep us safe. It's what they do. A couple of them are on the church board who are in complete agreement with this."

"They are? That's unusual, isn't it?" Artis shifted slightly. "Aidan, what do I do with my furniture?"

"You could sell it. You could give it to someone in need. Or there is a charity that takes in furniture for people who need it and can't afford to buy it."

"Oh, I like that idea. Who do we talk to?" Artis turned to face him and found him reaching to kiss her.

Chapter 16

Monday found Aidan walking back into his work office. He dropped his keys on the desk and looked around. He stared at the file folders stacked on it and sighed. Aidan didn't want to be there. He wanted to be with Artis. He had kissed her that morning and hugged her for a long time before walking away. Artis had locked the door behind him and that had given him some sense of peace.

Lyle stood outside of Aidan's office, watching his friend and fellow detective. He shook his head before he headed past to another office. He was due for a meeting that he had to be at. Lyle would be back later to assess how Aidan was.

Aidan looked up hours later and sighed. He had been deep into his work until Lyle had appeared in his office, his hand reaching to close the folder that Aidan had open in front of him.

"It's time you went home, Aidan." Lyle's voice was stern yet held compassion.

"Is it? I was deep into this." Aidan sat back, his eyes on his supervisor. "Lyle, where does our investigation stand?"

"Not where we want it to. We are missing a piece of information that we need." Lyle was frustrated at that.

"It's always that way, isn't it?" Aidan bit at his lip, a sign that he was unsure about something. "I talked to Emma Finlay."

"She's been in touch already, Aidan. No big deal. She said that you had a list of names that you gave her?"

"We do." Aidan reached for a folder that he had set to one side. "This is it. It's Artis' friends from her home town. She's put them in order of how close they were to one another. It really bothered her to do this. She also put in a list of coworkers from her former employment." Aidan paused at that. "I wonder if it's one of them."

"It's possible. Aidan, did she mention being threatened by anyone?"

Aidan thought back through the conversations that he had had with Artis before he shook his head.

"She didn't pinpoint anyone but there were a few that she hesitated about. She's marked them for you."

"She's ahead of us, then. That's good to know. Now, let's get you home. There's an officer ready to follow you."

Aidan nodded, tidied away his work, and rose to his feet. His head was aching, he had to admit, and he felt ready to crash. He was also ready to find Artis and to convince himself that she was all right and had not disappeared over the day.

Artis turned from the back door as she heard the front door open and close and then the sound of Aidan walking towards her. Both of their mothers had appeared over the morning, just to pray with her and to reassure themselves that she was fine.

—

Bridy had had a long conversation with her daughter that day. Now that Artis was no longer in their town, they were looking at moving as well. Not to Oak City, Bridy stated, but to a smaller town outside of there. Artis had simply hugged her mother, knowing that if she had stayed in her home town, her parents not likely would have moved.

"Have a good day, sweetheart?" Aidan simply held her for a moment, sensing that they both needed those few moments.

"I did. Mom and your mom were here. I have no idea where our fathers were. Mom muttered something about them being together doing whatever." She poked him as he snickered. "It's not funny. You have no idea what my Dad can dream up."

"If he's like my Dad, I have a good idea." Aidan bit at his lip. "Have you had lunch yet?"

"No, I was waiting for you." Artis waited for him to let her go. "Aidan? I can't get us a meal if you don't move."

Aidan grinned at her.

"I know, sweetheart. How be I change and then we head for Ben's? Hiding isn't going to solve this."

"I know. I want to be out and about but I worry about bringing danger to others."

"It will happen no matter where we are or who we're with. That's already been proven."

"I know. I just worry about it." Artis shoved away from him. "Go and change, Aidan. Let's make some plans too about how we bring this to a quick resolution."

"I want that too, sweetheart, but I also don't want you to be hurt or killed." Aidan walked away, leaving a sober Artis staring after him.

"I don't want that either, my love, but God is in control. I don't want to lose you now that I've found you."

Ben watched as Aidan entered the diner, Artis tight to his side. He nodded. It was true then, he decided. Aidan was having one of those adventures that the young people seemed to think that they needed to have. Paul, one of Don's team, had been around and asked that Ben keep an ear out for rumours on the street. Paul had been taken in by Ben when he found himself on the streets after being in foster care during his teens.

"Aidan?" Ben approached him, sliding into the booth across from the couple.

"Ben?" Aidan grinned at Ben. "This is my bride, Artis."

"I heard that you were married. Welcome to our family, Artis." Ben continued to watch the pair and saw the discomfort that briefly flickered across the lady's face. "Word is out on the streets, Aidan. Everyone is looking out for you two. If I hear anything, you know that I will find you or one of your fellow officers."

"I know that, Ben. You have done that in the past. As for Artis, I need to come up with some way

—

to protect her. She can't stay locked up in the house all the time. I'm back to work part time for now."

"We'll look after your lady, Aidan. Artis, this is your safe spot. If you are down town and become afraid, head here. The people on the street will watch out for you and make sure that you get here in safety. There are also undercover police officers who will watch out for you."

"Thank you, Ben. But I have to ask. Have you heard anything at all?" Artis was hopeful that he had and drew in a quivering breath when Ben shook his head.

Chapter 17

Two weeks later, Artis wandered through the small shops in the down town area. She needed to work but had been reluctant to do so. She had just come from an interview at a private clinic that worked with young people who were facing court. Artis was familiar with that line of work. She just wasn't sure that she wanted to do that again but she had to do something.

Frowning at her phone, Artis paused her steps. Don's sister, Daci, had reached out to her, asking that they meet for a meal. Daci ran the women's shelter and wanted to talk to her about possibly coming on staff. Her experience would certainly make Daci's life easier with the youths that came through the shelter.

Her head nodding, Artis looked up and then headed for Ben's. She didn't see the two men who were approaching her with evil intent on their faces. She also didn't see the men and women who stepped inbetween the men and Artis, preventing her from disappearing once more. Artis would hear of this afterwards.

Daci hugged Artis as she stopped in front of her. She studied the other lady, nodding to herself. Don was right. Artis was struggling emotionally. Daci had seen it all too often

"Artis? Are you okay with eating here?"

"It's okay. I just feel uncomfortable today. I want to be working. I'm just not sure if I would be safe anywhere."

"Come work with me. We have security on site. We need someone just like you. I have reached out to the community at times but having a child protection work on staff would help. The mothers and their families would not have to be put at risk going out into the community for appointments. We try to keep that risk down as much as we can." Daci made a quick decision. "Did you drive today?"

Artis had a sheepish look on her face.

"No, I walked. I know that I shouldn't have but I needed that." Artis frowned at Daci. "What are you asking?"

"I am asking you to grab something for lunch and then come with me. We can eat at the shelter and I'll tell you all about your new position." Daci yanked open the diner door and was through it before Artis had a chance to close her mouth.

Artis walked through the shelter, a thoughtful look on her face. She had asked for time to pray it over and to discuss it with Aidan. Her feeling was that she would take the work offered to her.

Daci approached her at last, keys in her hands.

"Ready to go, Artis?"

"I am. Thank you for the opportunity. I'll let you know as soon as I can."

"That's not a problem. Some of our funding comes from The Barnabas Foundation. The board there prays over a new position that they want to create. Then they pray for a person or couple to take it on. They approach that person or couple, offer it to them, and then tell them to pray over it. They do not set a time line for a response. I like that philosophy. Take your time to pray over it and discuss it with Aidan and whoever else that you need to." Daci reached to hug Artis. "Now, let's get you home."

Artis found her favourite seat in the sun room that evening, a mug of tea wrapped in her hands. She had been quiet over their meal, setting Aidan to send her questioning glances but he didn't speak. She looked up at Aidan as he sat beside her and then snuggled closer to him. They were content to sit and not speak.

Aidan began to pray, sensing that Artis was worrying over a problem. He just didn't know if she would share with him.

"Daci offered me a position at the shelter today." Artis turned to watch Aidan, finding him nodding. "Aidan?"

"That doesn't surprise me, sweetheart. I knew that she was looking for someone. What did you say?"

"That I wanted to pray about it and talk to you."

"That's only fair. She would have expected you to do that." Aidan's voice died down as he thought through the ramifications of what the work entailed.

"Have you heard anything, Aidan?" Artis was praying that this adventure was over.

—

"No, I haven't. I didn't think that I would. Whoever it is has stayed quiet. We're working on it as is Emma. She's been called in on some urgent investigations and has to set ours aside even though she has an employee working on it." Aidan settled back into his seat, drawing Artis closer to him.

Artis sighed. It was about what she had expected to hear.

"How do we do this then? We can't keep having people trail us around forever."

"No, we can't. I know that it's frustrating, sweetheart. We just need one person to come forward or we get that one piece of evidence that will crack it open. We won't stop living. We'll go out on dates, for walks, and visit our friends and families."

"It's called living, isn't it? And you're right. We do need to do that." Artis yawned before her face turned into Aidan's shoulder and she slept.

Aidan looked down at her, a sad smile on his face even as he petitioned God to solve this and soon. He worried about his lady. His eyes closed and he too slept, the discussion that they needed to have not happening.

Artis' head raised during the night. She was sure that she heard movement in the house but that was not possible. Their security system had been set and it would have sounded an alarm if someone had entered the house. She roused further to reach for the blanket on the back of the couch, pulling it over them and then sleeping again.

Aidan was on his feet in the morning, dismayed and then frightened at Artis' words. He immediately went to the security feed and then pointed to the men outside their home.

"I recognize one of them. He was the one who shot you. Thank God they couldn't get in." Artis shook with fear for a moment. "They're getting desperate to get one of us, Aidan."

"They are. They want you for some reason. But they'll go after me to get to you. Our parents are safe for now, I would suspect. I pray that they are."

"Me too, Aidan. Me too. I don't know what I would do if one of them was hurt because of me." She sat silent for a moment. "We have both faced threats from our work, you more than me. I don't remember anyone ever threatening my family."

"I have not faced that. But it can happen. I have had colleagues who have had that happen to them. We need to plan how we live, sweetheart. We are not staying hidden. We will be out there and in the open." Aidan reached to hug her, knowing that he had to head out of the door in a few minutes. "We needed to talk last night and didn't get a chance."

"No, we didn't. I think the restless sleep that we have had finally caught up to us. "I'll be here when you get home. We'll talk this afternoon. I plan to spend the morning catching up on my studies. I have to do that to keep current with the laws."

"And you haven't taken the time to do that, have you?" He grinned at her before he kissed her and walked away, a whistle trailing behind him.

—

Artis followed after a few moments to lock the door behind him. A smile crossed her face. She loved and was loved in return. Life couldn't get better than that, she decided. Well, the only thing that would make it better would be to have their adventure solved. She reached for her bottle of water and headed for the office. Artis was soon lost in her studies, oblivious to the sounds around her.

A week later, Aidan walked through the down town area towards a crime scene. He had been cleared to return to work full time. Artis had simply looked at him and then walked away. Aidan knew that Artis was worried about him more now that he was back to work full time.

His eyes took in the crime scene. A nasty one, he could already tell. Not what he wanted for a mid-week crime. George looked around as well.

"This is brutal, Aidan."

"I know. Over the top." Aidan walked to the responding officers and just stood with them, waiting for them to speak.

"This is a strange one, Aidan. No one hated Old Bob." The officers had all taken care of the older homeless man. It had shocked them to find out that he had been murdered.

"They did, Tom. That they did. He looked after everyone and everyone looked after him." Aidan looked around at the crime scene tech who had approached him. "Tracy?"

"Aidan? This is directed at you!" Tracy was shocked to say the least, handing him an evidence bag.

"It is?" Aidan was shocked as well, reaching for the bag and then looking down at the roughly-scrawled letter in it. He read it and then passed it to George.

They shared a look before George read the letter. "I don't understand this."

"They're warning you, Aidan." George was saddened that death had come to trouble Aidan and Artis. "And wanting Artis."

"They are. And that worries me. Tom? Did anyone see anything>"

Tom shook his head. If someone had witnessed this, they were not speaking out. That told him that they were afraid of whoever had done the deed had caused great fear among the people on the streets.

Lyle watched Aidan closely as he sorted through the folders on his desk. George had gone to him when the two had returned to the office, explaining what had happened. Lyle had nodded and then headed for Aidan.

"Aidan? Talk to me." Lyle spoke at last, causing Aidan's head to raise as the younger man stared at his supervisor. He could hear the noise and talking outside of the closed office door.

"I don't know what to say, Lyle. I really don't. I hate this. Old Bob didn't deserve to be killed like this. And for what?"

"The "for what" is difficult to determine. They are warning you, Aidan. They will not hesitate to kill you if they need to. They want Artis. Yet, we don't know why or who as of now."

"We don't. And this is going to devastate her. She had met Old Bob on the weekend. He had spent time talking with her." Aidan paled. "That's why. They think that she may have said something or that he

—

said something." Aidan sat back in his chair, not sure what to think. His thoughts were jumbled at best.

"I would suspect that you are correct, Aidan." Lyle was on his feet. "Pack up what you need to work from home. I'm authorizing that. An officer will escort you home and stay there until he is relieved. You have that around the clock for the next week or so. If Artis goes out, she only does that with an escort." Lyle walked away, leaving Aidan staring after him.

Artis turned from the computer in the office as she heard the front door open and close and then heard Aidan's footsteps coming towards her. She was on her feet, moving into his hug. His arms tightened around her also too tight.

"Aidan? What are you doing home?" Artis looked up at him.

"I was sent home to work. We need to talk, Artis." His arm turned her to the couch where he pulled her down beside him. His head bowed as he prayed. He kept it bowed as he sought for words to explain to Artis what had happened.

"Something happened, Aidan. Tell me what." Artis was almost angry with him.

"There has been something happen. Old Bob was murdered overnight. It was a threat towards us." Aidan held Artis as she wept. "Lyle sent me to work from home. It's not the best situation but it's what we need to do. We can't go back and change that."

"I just talked with him. He shared his life story with me. I wish that it was different. What do we do now?"

"We work on solving this, for one thing. There is a patrol officer stationed outside. One will be there for the next week or so. Lyle also said that if you go out on your one, an officer goes with you."

"Goodbye, freedom." Artis was glum at Aidan's words. It was what they had discussed. She had prayed that it would not come to that but it had. "Where does the investigation stand?"

"I don't know, sweetheart. It is not my investigation and they can't tell me much. It's not how things are done."

"I know. I was just hoping that someone had said something." Artis thought through what little she knew. "How do we find this person or persons?"

"That's a good question, sweetheart. I know that George is working on it but he can't say much to me. And Emma is working it. She'll come up with something in the next day or so. It's what she does."

"I see. I want this over, Aidan. It's taking up too much of our lives. Who hates us this much?"

Aidan's hand stopped robbing at his jeans. The way that Artis had worded her question made him pause.

"Why did you word it that way?" Aidan studied her face, not sure what to think.

"They could have been following you. It never made sense why they shot you like they did. It was a warning but who were they warning?" Artis rubbed at her face with both hands. "I'm not wording it very well."

"No, you worded it correctly. I had just never thought of it that way. That changes how we work this."

"It does but not tonight. You're emotionally exhausted tonight, Aidan. You need to set aside whatever you're working on until tomorrow."

Aidan kissed his lady, thinking that she was so correct in her words. He did need to set aside his work until the next day.

—

Chapter 19

Aidan shuffled through the paperwork on his desk the next morning. He sighed. He wanted to be in the office with the give and take between the officers. It just wasn't happening. Aidan could hear Artis singing softly to herself in another room. She had simply taken her laptop and moved away to do some more studying. They were both still praying through the employment offer from Daci. It seemed as if Artis was leaning towards accepting it.

Artis raised her head at last, setting aside the laptop and stretching. Her head tilted as she heard Aidan on a call. She smiled. She liked having him around and not just for the security of that. The comfort from having him in the house was what she had been missing. She knew that it would change when he was able to go back to the office but by that time, she was praying that she would be back working at that point.

Walking through the house, Artis approached their front door, pausing to stare out of the window on the door. A marked patrol car sat at the curb and she could see the officer walking around the yard. She was afraid but could not put a finger on why she felt that way that day.

Aidan roused a couple of hours later, setting aside his work and then rising. He hunted for Artis, finding her back in front of the door. His arms wrapped around her and pulled her back against him.

"What's so interesting out there, sweetheart?"

—

Artis shrugged. She had no idea why she kept going back to the door and staring out of it. The patrol officer was still there, standing outside his car for now.

"I don't know, Aidan. The officer is out there. He's been around the house more than once."

"I see. He's just doing what he's trained to do." Aidan's head tilted so that he could study her face. "There's more to it than just that."

"There is. And I just don't know what or how to express myself. I don't usually have that trouble." Her elbow hit Aidan's ribs as he chuckled. "Stop laughing, buster."

"I'm sorry. You just sounded so matter of fact saying that. I know it's not you." Aidan turned her from the door and to the kitchen. "We'll figure it out, sweetheart. At some point, we'll figure it out."

"I know we will. I just want it to be today." Artis sighed as she heard the door bell ring. "Who's bothering us now?"

Aidan was laughing as he headed for the door. He sobered a bit as he saw Abe and Emma Finlay standing there.

"Abe? Emma? I didn't expect to see you two today." He reached to hug Emma and then to shake hands with Abe.

"No, we weren't planning on coming this way but we felt that we had to. Darcy came up with a profile that she wanted to get to you but they were heading the other way. She's done one for both of you. She's adamant that there are two different people involved." Emma studied her friend, seeing the stress that he was trying to hide.

"That's what we were just discussing. It doesn't make sense to have only one." He pointed towards the kitchen. "We were just about to eat. Come and join us." He walked to where Artis had stopped in the doorway, wrapping her into a hug. "Artis, sweetheart. This is Abe and Emma. They had a profile for us."

"A profile? Does she do that do?" Artis was confused for a moment as the others laughed and felt uncomfortable.

"It's okay, Artis. A friend of ours is a retired forensics psychologist. She does profiles for friends. She has prepared profiles for both you and Aidan. But first, what can I do to help you with your meal?"

"It's just sandwiches. I'm sorry." Artis looked at the bread and sandwich fixings, thinking that it was not much to offer.

"It's okay, Artis. We're not fussy. Sandwiches are just fine. We didn't realize that it was so close to a meal time or we would have waited." She frowned as she heard the door bell and then Aidan's surprised voice.

"Artis? We can put the sandwich stuff away. Ben just sent over four orders of his fish and chips." Aidan held up the bag. "He heard that Abe and Emma were heading this way. And no, I don't know how he finds out these things."

"He's like my Uncle Mac." Abe reached to help set out their meal. "Mac can remember what you order one time and then you never have to tell him again unless you want something different.”

The meal over and the table cleaned up, Abe hesitated before he looked at the other couple. Emma’s hand covered his for a moment.

“I would like to pray for you, Aidan and Artis. It’s what we do. We pray for our friends before we start going over any evidence or information that we want to share with them.”

“Thank you, Abe.” Artis spoke up, not waiting for Aidan to agree. “It’s what my parents do and I’m used to that.”

Abe raised his head almost an hour later, his eyes on Emma. She nodded at him. His gaze then went to Aidan and Artis. That couple were waiting for him to speak.

“Aidan. Artis. We have been working on this as we can. I have employees working on it as well.” Emma handed over the folder. “This is what we have so far. Read through it and then we’ll talk.”

Artis reached for the folder, setting it down and then opening it. Aidan’s arm was around her. She began to read, Aidan’s head close to hers. They were astounded at what Emma had discovered, although Aidan had expected that from her.

“Emma? I don’t understand how you did this.” Artis looked up at last, a frown on her face.

“I can’t explain how I find the information that I do. But God always leads me to what I need for each case. This is what He has given me for you.” Emma hesitated for a moment. "Artis, we feel strongly that it is someone from your previous office who is behind what happened to you. Did you sense anything about them?"

Artis shook her head. That was a thought that had not crossed her mind. She turned to Aidan to see a look on his face that said he had.

"Aidan?"

"Artis? It could well be someone from your old office. Now for me? It could be anyone."

"That's true, Aidan." Abe spoke up. "We've seen that before. Our friends from the police force in Riverville would be good to speak with. We can arrange a meal this weekend and have you speak with them."

"That would work." Aidan hesitated, not sure how they would get there.

"I can speak with Don and his team and see if we can get them to help. Or else Richard might step in."

"That would work." Aidan sighed. "This is not how today should be."

"It never is, Aidan. We know that only too well. I know that my team will share their stories with you, Artis. It helps to know that you aren't alone in all this." Abe grinned at her for a moment.

"We're not? And just how many people do you know who have gone through something?" She looked at him, not expecting to hear his answer.

"Dozens, Artis. Dozens. Not just our family and friends but people that we were asked to help." Abe shrugged. "I run a security team, Artis. We do training now but at one time we were out there on the front lines protecting people. That goes for Don and Richard as well." Abe reached to touch her hand. "We will not walk away from you. We will do our best to protect you. And Emma will continue to research what she can. Once she's proven it, she will pass it on to the investigators here. And if necessary, she will turn it over to the investigator in your home town."

Aidan closed and locked the door after Abe and Emma. His head dropped for a moment. He was exhausted but Artis needed him. He heard her soft footsteps stop in front of him and a gentle hand touched his head before she simply hugged him. He turned them to the back deck, twilight dropping down, and found their favourite seats. Aidan bowed his head and began to pray for his lady, begging God's protection on them both.

Chapter 20

Dodging the drops of rain, Aidan ran for Ben's diner, pulling open the door and then approaching Ben. Ben looked up and then pointed towards his office. Aidan nodded and headed that way, taking with thanks the tray that was handed to him. He found a seat and began to eat the lunch provided for him. Aidan was grateful for the meal. He had not had time to eat that day and he was starved.

Ben stood in the hallway, watching Aidan closely. He was wearing out, Ben decided, and needed a break. He sighed to himself. Ben wanted this over for Aidan and his bride. Only, it didn't seem as if that would happen any time soon.

Ben slumped into his desk chair, staring at the work that he needed to get to. Only he never seemed to have the time to do so.

Aidan looked up, a frown on his face. Something was going on with Ben and he wished to help him if he could.

"Ben? You wanted to speak with me?"

"I did, Aidan. And now I don't know how to do just that." Ben rubbed at his face, his eyes on Aidan. "It's about what you two are going through. I have been given information for you. It needs to be verified, of course, but it might explain why." Ben handed over a large brown envelope.

Aidan took it, a look on his face that expressed hope that this might be over.

———

"What is this, Ben?" Aidan peeked into the envelope, a frown on his face.

"I was told that you needed this. It will help move forward the investigation or so I'm told. I have not looked at it. And the person who handed it to me didn't tell me what it was." Ben nodded at the envelope. "I pray that it does just that."

"Thank you, Ben." Aidan fingered the envelope, wanting to look at it but knowing that he couldn't right at the moment. He tucked it inside his jacket and then walked away, leaving Ben staring after him.

Artis moved into Aidan's space that afternoon and into his hug. She was surprised to see him home early.

"Aidan? You're early?"

"I am. I have an envelope to open with you. Ben gave it to me this afternoon." Aidan kissed her and then watched her face as she studied him in return.

"Aidan? When does this end?" Artis had been afraid all day and could not tell why. She just felt as if everything was closing in on them and there was nothing that they could do to prevent it.

"I am praying that it is over soon, sweetheart. I know. We keep saying that. There is just one piece of information that we need to solve this. And we don't have that yet. Unless it's in the envelope that Ben handed me." He reached for her hand, drawing her to the outdoors. Even though it was still drizzling, their favourite chairs were sheltered. He shoved her into hers and then sat beside her, reaching for her hand.

———

106

"We need to cover one another in prayer. It's coming to a time when it will be dangerous for us."

"I know. That's what everyone is saying. I am just so afraid, Aidan, that someone else will be hurt because of us."

"I know. I feel the same." Aidan's head dropped. He really had no idea what to say to her.

Artis watched him before she was on her feet, returning with the envelope. She stared at the writing that scrawled Aidan's name across it. She didn't recognize it.

"Do you recognize the writing?" Artis was hopeful that he did.

Aidan shook his head.

"No, I don't. I wish that I did. I'd find that person and talk to them." He reached for the envelope, fingering it before he worked to open the flap. He raised his eyes to stare towards the back of the yard. He was afraid, he decided, and uncertain as to what the future was holding for them.

Aidan drew out the paperwork and photos that were in the envelope. He stared down at it for a moment before Artis reached for it. She sorted through it, setting the photos to one side before she began to read the paperwork. She passed each page off to Aidan as she finished it. He took each one and read it.

Artis frowned as she finished reading the paperwork, not sure what to think.

"This doesn't make any sense, Aidan. Who are they talking about? It doesn't sound like us."

"No, it doesn't. I wonder who it is. They don't give any names. This is just too bizarre." Aidan set the paperwork to one side and reached for the photos. He flipped through them before he paused at the last one.

"This is us at the diner, Artis." He handed it back to her. "I don't recognize the people in the other photos. Do you?"

Artis reached for them, looking through them as well.

"No, I don't. Who are these people? What did Ben say?" Artis eyed Aidan for a moment, finding him shaking his head.

"He didn't say anything. I'll need to talk to him again about who it was that left these for us." Aidan sighed. "This doesn't help us right now."

Artis reached for the photos, snapping her own copies of them, and then sending them all on to Emma.

"I've sent them to Emma. She might be able to help." She tucked away her phone before taking back the paperwork. "I wish this was over and that this would help to do that. It doesn't seem to be moving it along."

Aidan was on his feet, heading for the front door. His parents stood there as did Artis' parents.

"You are here?" Aidan was puzzled at that.

"We are, son. We need to talk with you. We might have some information." Alin looked past Aidan at Artis. "Artis? What are you waving at us?" He grinned at her.

"These. Ben handed this paperwork and photos to Aidan today. We don't know who they are but maybe you do?" Artis was hopeful that they did.

Chapter 21

Alin took the paperwork, his eyes on his son and then his son's bride. Something was going on with those two that he wasn't sure about. He would wait until they spoke to him.

Aidan reached to hug the mothers before he pointed towards the office. His hand found Artis', who clung to him. His eyes searched her face before he nodded. She trusted him and that was something for him to digest at some point. Just not now.

"Artis? What can we do for you?" Ardeen wrapped an arm around the younger woman.

Bridy shared a look with Ardeen, both of the mothers worried about the lady.

"I don't know what to say, Ardeen. I really don't." Artis drew in a deep breath that was almost a sob.

"Well then, we just do what we need to for both you and Aidan." Bridy's arms surrounded her daughter. This was one thing that she couldn't make right for her daughter, not any more. It was not the same as when Artis was young and problems were easy to solve. All she could do was beg God to protect her daughter and her groom.

Bayne reached for the paperwork that Aidan was holding, not sure what was going on. He read through them, handing them off to Alin as he finished each page.

"Son? What is this?" Alin looked at his son, finding Aidan watching Artis.

Aidan shrugged. He had a sense of what it was but he wasn't completely sure.

"I don't know, Dad. I was given that parcel by Ben. There are photos as well. The only one that we recognize anyone in? It's the last one that's of Artis and me. I know when it was taken. It was taken three days ago when we went to Ben's for a meal." Aidan was distraught but trying hard to hide it from their parents.

"I recognize these people." Bayne held up a photo. "They're from our town but are not really prominent. They stay in the background. I was never sure if they were in crime or not."

Bridy reached for the photo, a frown on her face as she studied it. She sighed. *Lord, I know these people and have for years. I have always had a sense of fear around them. They watched Artis too closely over the years. I could never understand why. It grew worse, Lord, as she began to work in her chosen line. I am glad, Lord, that she is not in our town any more and that she has Aidan to protect her. These two are in love with one another. They are just who You chose for one another.*

"This couple, Aidan? They were always watching Artis. I could never understand why. We kept her away from them as much as we could. Ed and Lou White? That's who they are. I don't know if they are into crime or not. However, I did see them watching Artis more and more in the last few years."

Bridy turned to her daughter. "Did you ever see them around you?"

Artis shook her head. She had never seen the couple that she could remember.

"I don't know them, Mom. What did they do in town?"

"I'm not really sure, Artis. They never seemed to have a source of income. And they had no family who would have left them a fortune. We could never understand how they managed to live." She reached for the rest of the photos, giving names to them all. "Aidan, these are from our town. I don't know how they are related but I think that I had heard they were."

Aidan nodded. It had come to that point, he decided, that George may need to head to that town. He wanted to go with him, if he did, but knew that he could not. He felt Artis shifting beside him and looked down at her. He saw the fear that she was trying hard to hide. *Lord, be with my lady. Give her the peace that she needs right now. Let her feel Your protection and care. And please help us to solve this quickly. I don't want to see it prolonged.*

Artis reached for the photos again, recognizing the background now that her mother had named the people.

"These were taken recently, weren't they?"

"They were, Artis. You can see some of the decorations for the festival that was just held. They are watching you closely, Artis." Bayne was worried about his daughter and her groom. He just knew that something else would be happening to them. He feared that they would be killed.

"We'll take all the precautions that we can, Bayne. But life has a way of happening and we can't predict what other people do. We've seen it way too often." Aidan had been to his share of assaults, attempted murders, and murders over the years. He didn't want to become one of those statistics or see Artis become one.

"That's how life works, Aidan. You have seen it, I know." Alin watched his son closely, praying for him. He really wasn't sure how to pray at this point but he was confident that his prayers would reach to his Heavenly Father who already knew the path that his son and bride would walk.

"Dad? The paperwork? Do you have any idea about it? It's bizarre. I know that George and Lyle will take it but it was given to us." Aidan was puzzled by the paperwork. It really didn't make sense. It was more gibberish, he decided, than anything.

"They're not telling you anything or asking you anything. Their statements don't correlate very well with one another. You are correct when you state that it doesn't make any sense."

Artis reached to take the paperwork back. A thought had come to her and she needed to follow it. She was on her feet to make copies of the papers and then tucked the originals back into the envelope which she set to one aside. Handing out the copies, she looked around in surges as she saw Don and his wife,

Delanie, appear. She had not heard the doorbell but Alin had and had gone to open the door.

"Don?"

"We're here, Artis, here to help. What do you have?" He took the photos and then the copy of the paperwork, a frown on his face as he studied Aidan. "Aidan?"

Aidan sighed to himself. Don would help, he knew. He just didn't know how far it would go that day in determining what was going on.

"Ben handed me these today. Bayne and Bridy have recognized the people in the photos from their town. It's the paperwork that is very strange."

Don nodded and read through the copy that he held. He looked up, puzzled.

"This is bizarre, Aidan. It is definitely not making any sense." Don looked at Delanie as she made a sound. "Delanie?"

"I think it's in code of some kind. We just have to figure that out." She had a pen out and was concentrating on the paperwork before Don could even respond.

Artis was nodding. That had been her thought. She moved to sit beside Delanie, the mothers joining them as they worked through the papers.

Bayne grinned as he saw that.

"The race is on, fellows. The ladies want to beat us in solving it. Up for a challenge?" His grin widened

as the men responded by reaching for their own copies
of the papers.

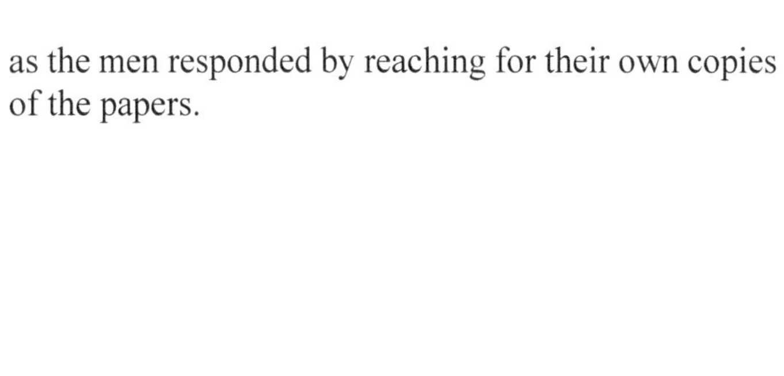

Chapter 22

Aidan was on his feet a couple of hours later, heading for the kitchen. Don was beside him, knowing that Aidan was likely heading to find them something to eat. They worked together to prepare a meal just as they had many times in the past.

"Aidan? What are your thoughts?" Don's voice broke into the silence of the room.

"I don't know what to think, Don. I think Delanie has the right idea about the paperwork. Bridy has identified the people in the photos. George will need all that." Aidan sighed before he rubbed at his head. He had a headache developing that he knew would only grow worse with time.

"It could well be a code. Or it could just be a bunch of gibberish to throw off the investigation." Don reached for a tray to set the food on before he turned to watch Aidan. "It could be that. We've seen that before." Don paused for a moment. "What more can we do for you and Artis?"

Aidan shrugged, his hand resting on the off-white granite countertop. He studied the room, seeing the little touches that Artis had been adding that made it feel more like a home and not just a house to live in.

"I don't know, Don. You are all doing so much." He looked around as he sensed another presence. "George?"

"I had to come, Aidan. God told me to." George was puzzled at the strong urge that he had felt to come to Aidan's.

"I'm glad. We have some information for you. But first, we plan on eating and then spending time in prayer." Aidan walked away with a tray, leaving Don shrugging as George looked at him.

"Don? What is this about?" George stared between the door and Don.

"Ben handed Aidan some paperwork and photos. Bayne and Bridy have identified the people in the photos from their home town. The paperwork seems to be a bunch of gibberish. Delanie has an idea that the paperwork might be in code of some kind. They're working on that. I don't know that she's right but we'll see."

"Gibberish? Code? Just what are you talking about?" George headed for the office, stopping as Artis met him in the hallway and shoved papers at him. "Artis?"

"This. These are copies of what Ben gave Aidan. You need them." She turned and almost ran back into the office.

George could feel the fear emanating from her. He wanted this over for his friends. He just didn't know if that would work very quickly. Their case was going cold. He prayed that the paperwork he held would advance it. Somehow, he didn't think that it would.

An hour later, George reached for the photos. Bayne and Bridy had written the names of the people on the back of each photo as well as what they knew about each one. That would help. He snapped copies of each side of each photo and sent them on to Emma. She would work with that, he knew, and find out what she could on each person.

"Aidan. Talk to me. Tell me what you think." George shared a look with Aidan who nodded.

"What do I think? My first impression was that it was a red herring, something to throw us off. But when Bayne and Bridy identified the people, then I knew that this was not just an unrelated incident. We need to look into it. I know that you will as you can. We'll work it but hand over anything that we find for you to verify."

George nodded, knowing that Aidan was correct. He would need to verify everything. He read through the paperwork, seeing what Aidan had meant. The words didn't mean a lot. He frowned. He had seen something like this before. He just had to remember when and where and he would do that.

"Aidan?" Bayne looked up, a frown on his face. "The second page? If you take every fifth word, it makes sense."

Everyone stared at him before they were flipping to that page and underlying the words. Artis paled as she read what it said.

"Dad? Mom? Is this for real?" Artis was shaking with fear. Aidan moved to sit beside her, wrapping an arm around her. She leaned back against him, struggling to control her emotions.

Bayne nodded, knowing how it would affect his daughter. It was a threat, out in the open. He sighed to himself. They needed to find who this was and then have them put behind bars. He continued to work through the papers, going back to the first page and sorting out what it really said.

"The first page explains why this was given to you, Aidan. The third page explains how the man or woman came upon it. The fourth page gives details of who it is. The fifth page is simply a summary of what the person knows."

George had finished his own assessment of what was hidden. Bayne was spot on with his words, he decided. Now he had to track down whoever this was. That meant he had to speak with Ben. He was on his feet, stepping outside as he called Ben.

"Ben? It's George." George heard a door close and knew that Ben had closed the door to his office. "That paperwork that you gave to Aidan? Where did you get it?"

"The envelope? It just appeared with a note asking that I hand it to Ben. I think I saw who left it but I'm not sure." Ben didn't want to accuse anyone without proof.

"What about your security feed? Does it show whoever it was?" George walked rapidly to his car and drove away, heading for Ben's diner.

Ben was waiting for George, knowing full well that George would appear. He pointed to his computer.

"There. There's your person. I can't tell if it's a man or woman though. They've disguised themselves. I have a copy of it on a thumb drive for you." Ben handed it over.

"Thanks, Ben." George studied the video and agreed with Ben. It was hard to identify who it was but there was something familiar about the person and their walk. He prayed that he could remember who it was.

Chapter 23

The next day, Artis turned back from the front door. She had planned on going out but something stopped her from opening the door. She moved to stare out of the living room window, a frown on her face. Artis stared at the car that was parked in front of her house. It had been there all morning. She didn't like it.

Aidan approached her from where he had been working in the office and wrapped her into a hug.

"Something wrong, sweetheart?"

"There is. That car has been there all morning. I don't recognize it." Artis pointed at the car. "Do you recognize it?"

"No, I can't say that I do." Aidan tilted his head to read the plate. "Let me call it in." He did that, a sigh of relief coming to him as he heard the owner's name. "It's okay, sweetheart. It's a friend. He works for a security team and his boss likely sent him to watch over us."

Aidan walked towards the car, finding the man stepping out.

"Timothy? Richard send you?" Aidan reached to shake Timothy's hand as Timothy grinned at him.

"He did. Stephen's around here as well. Naomi and Silver are at the office and working on what they can. Don was in touch. He can't be here but he knew that we were free this week." Timothy looked past

Aidan as Artis approached. "Introduce me to your lady."

Aidan grinned as he wrapped an arm around her.

"This is my bride, Artis. Artis? This is a friend from Greenton. He works on a security team. Richard and Don are friends and Don reached out to him."

"Hi. You scared me." Artis glared as Timothy grinned at her. "Do you always do that?"

"Not usually, but sometimes we do. We don't mean to." Timothy looked around as he heard footsteps. "Stephen, this is Aidan's bride, Artis. Artis, this is Stephen, a coworker of mine."

Artis turned her glare towards Stephen as he grinned at her.

"What is it with you two? You both should be ashamed of yourselves."

Aidan's arm tightened around Artis as he tried to hide his own grin. That earned him a glare as well.

"Aidan!" Artis shoved at him but he refused to let her go.

"It's okay, sweetheart. They're here for now to protect us. Now, how be we head into the house, fellows? You can tell us what you have discovered so far. And just where is Richard?"

"He's with Don, working through some logistics of what we need to do." Stephen hesitated for a moment. "We think that you will need us in the near future and we want to be prepared for any eventuality that may arise. And you can help us with the planning. We need to know your schedules.”

Artis snorted at that, causing the men to grin once more.

“I don’t have a schedule. I just do what I need to when I need to. Aidan on the other hand does have a schedule, whether it’s at the office or at home. I don’t work at present.”

“That’s what Don said. He also said that you used to work as a youth protection worker. How does that play into this?” Timothy shared a look with Aidan who shrugged.

“I don’t know and I wish that I did. I want this over, guys. Aidan needs to get back his life.”

“But you’re not sure if you’re the target or he is? Is that how I’m reading this?” Timothy nodded at Aidan, seeing the closed look on the other man’s face.

“That’s about the size of it. Now, how do we do this?” Artis reached for the coffee pot, Aidan handing her mugs. “It’s lunchtime, do you know that?”

Timothy began to laugh. Artis was good for Aidan, he decided. She would challenge him but support him. That’s what all their wives did.

“We’ve been through stuff like this, Artis. So we have a sense of what you are facing.” He nodded as she spun to stare at Timothy. “All of us. Richard’s team. Don’s team. Abe’s team. And many friends. Those friends include Toryn. Even as chief of police, he was not immune to this.”

Artis spun to stare at Stephen. She had not been expecting to hear that. She glared at Aidan as he laughed before he hugged her.

"Draw in the claws, sweetheart. They survived and are in love with their spouses. God worked through them to bring people to justice."

"And He couldn't do it any other way? Is that what you're saying why we're going through this?" Artis moved away from Aidan, opening the fridge and pulling out a bottle of water. "I don't want to do this."

Timothy and Stephen shared a look. Artis needed to talk with Silver and Naomi.

"None of us did, Artis. Not one of us. But we survived. God protected us. It didn't mean that we didn't go through stuff that we didn't want to. But He received the glory that was due to Him because of our faith and how we were witnesses for Him." Timothy relived for a moment what he and Tate had gone through.

Artis had turned to watch him. Her brows were lowered in a frown. She didn't understand why God allowed adventures and dangers. She just knew that she had to trust Him. And at times that was very hard to do.

"Timothy? How did you do it?" Artis pulled out a chair, desperate to hear his story.

"With God's guidance and protection. With the help of my team and my friends. It was not easy. The police chief in our town? He walked into a road house to rescue his lady and married her the next day to keep her safe. Andrew's Phoebe thought that she was a cousin of Toryn's only to find out that she's not A detective friend? His first wife was killed by a drug dealer. His second wife? Her groom was killed on their wedding day. He was into drugs and was killed to keep him quiet. So you see? It doesn't matter if we're in law enforcement of some kind or not or just the average citizen. God works in our lives to bring crime to an end and the offenders to justice. I know that He never leaves us, forsakes us, or forgets us. He has our names written on the palms of His hands."

Aidan was nodding as was Stephen.

"I think that we need to get together with your team, Timothy. Artis needs to hear your stories and hear how God protected you all."

"We'll get together. Are you two free on Saturday?" Stephen knew that his team had planned a meal together on Saturday. "Andrew and Bill are sharing a meal with us. And our pastor, Silas and his wife, Madigan, will be there. They had an adventure as well."

"That works, Stephen. We'll head your way mid-morning." Aidan's eyes were on Artis, seeing relief in her eyes as she realized that she was not alone in this.

Chapter 24

Saturday morning found Artis pacing the house. Aidan was on a call that he hadn't wanted to take, a followup call to one of his investigations. She reached for the package of papers and photos that they had prepared the night before to take with them. Artis was praying that somehow today might make a difference in the investigation. Richard's wife, Raleigh, had reached out to Artis the day before, just to confirm that Artis and Aidan would be there on Saturday.

Raleigh had taken time to pray with Artis, something that Artis had appreciated. Aidan had walked into the room at the end of the conversation, finding Artis in tears. He had wrapped her in his arms and prayed for her, a kiss on her cheek when he finished.

Aidan knew that this was coming to a more dangerous time for them. He had had a heart-to-heart talk with both sets of parents, laying it out for them as to what he expected to happen. They had not been surprised at his words, only more worried. They promised to be as careful as they could be, knowing that to reach Aidan and Artis, the men might go after the parents.

Aidan finally tucked away his phone, his head dropping for a moment. He scrawled out his notes from the call, tucked them away in his safe, and then headed for Artis.

"Artis? Are you sure that you're ready to meet these friends? I can call and cancel. They'd understand."

Artis turned to face him, not sure what to say. She knew that he would do just that but she needed to do this.

"I'm sure, I think, Aidan." She groaned as he grinned at her. "I know. Very definite, isn't it? I just have this fear about today, that if we go, we won't come home." She leaned against him, feeling his strength of character as he held her.

"We go with God's protection, sweetheart. If He allows something to happen, then that is in His will for us. He doesn't want anything but good for us."

"I know. It's easy to say the words at times but so hard to believe them and follow them." Artis stepped away from him and reached for her purse. "Are you all set?"

"I am." Aidan reached for her hand, stopping to pray for them before he locked the door behind him and tucked her into his truck.

Richard paced the sidewalk in front of his home. He kept glancing at his watch. It was well past time for Aidan and Artis to have arrived and they had not. Andrew and Bill stood nearby, not saying much but knowing how Richard thought, they too were worried.

"Richard? No word from Aidan?" Bill spoke at last.

———

"Not a word. He should have been here by now. And if he was delayed, he would have called or at last sent a text to one of us."

Bill and Andrew shared a look before Bill headed for his car. Andrew was beside him. Richard knew just what they were up to. He sighed. This was not good. He looked down at his phone, not seeing a message from Aidan. And there should be.

Andrew searched the side of the road as Bill headed for Oak City. The hour-long drive seemed to take forever. Bill parked at Aidan's home and saw that Aidan's truck was gone. The two men walked around Aidan's home and checked the doors.

"They must have left, Andrew. I didn't see anything on the road. Did you?"

"No, and I would have thought that we should have. Now, let's head back. I'll give Toryn a call and see if he's heard from Aidan."

Toryn was shocked to hear that Aidan seemed to have disappeared. He had been relaxing at home, taking a rare day to just do nothing. On his feet, he headed for his own truck, knowing that he could not just sit at home and wait. Slaney was off with the ladies from Don's team and also Don's sister, Daci.

Lyle was shocked as well and simply walked out of the office to start searching. George walked beside him. They too headed out to search for Aidan and Artis even as it went out over the police radio that Aidan was missing. Consternation spread through the force.

———

Andrew's eyes watched the edge of the road. His sudden yell startled Bill.

"To the side there, Bill." Andrew was out of the truck and running down through the ditch and then up through the tall grass and weeds, following the track marks across the area. He slid to a stop, a hand reaching out to touch the truck.

Bill slammed the truck into park and was running after Andrew. A quick glance confirmed that the license plate was Aidan's.

"Any sign of them, Andrew?" Bill was on the other side of the truck, pulling open the passenger door. No one was inside of the truck. He saw a purse on the floor and reached for it, confirming that it was Artis'.

"Where are they, Bill?" Andrew had wrenched open the driver's door and stood, shock on his face for a moment before he reached for his phone. It was not in his jurisdiction but was that of the county force. Andrew had been a lieutenant on that force before he took over the position of police chief in Greenton.

"Not here." Bill moved back, stepping carefully. He searched the area and then pointed. "There. Those are more than two sets of footprints."

Andrew and Bill leaned against his truck thirty minutes later. They watched closely as the county force set about the investigation. One of the officers approached them.

"Andrew? Bill? What's the story? Dispatch said that it was one of the detectives from Oak City, Aidan McNeill."

"It is. He's missing as is his wife, Artis. Someone has been targeting them. In fact, Aidan was injured not that long again after being kidnapped." Andrew's voice was stern. He was more than worried about his friends.

"He was? I heard that something was going on with him." The officer moved away, leaving Andrew and Bill to wait.

Andrew's phone was out as it chimed.

"Toryn?" Andrew's voice was flat as he answered Toryn's call.

"Where are you, Andrew?"

"About thirty minutes out of Oak City. We have the truck but not Aidan or Artis." Andrew gave a sudden shout, tucking his phone away despite Toryn's protests. He was running away from the truck, heading for a strand of trees. Bending over, he reached for the body. It was Aidan.

"Andrew?" Bill knelt beside him, calling back that they needed paramedics.

"He's alive, Bill. He's been knocked out. Where's Artis?"

Bill was on his feet, looking around but being careful not to disturb anything. He could hear the sounds of sirens and then the noise of footsteps moving towards them. He turned as Andrew stood beside him, Toryn appearing as well.

———

"Guys? What do we know?" Toryn's eyes were on Aidan. He was more than worried about his detective.

"Not a lot. We just found him. Artis isn't around unless she's hidden somewhere else." Andrew watched as Toryn moved away to speak with one of the responding officers.

"I don't like this, Andrew." Bill looked around, desperate to find Artis. He frowned and then walked about twenty feet away before he was calling for help. He had found Artis but like Aidan, she was unmoving.

Chapter 25

Alin and Ardeen ran for the hospital entrance to find Bayne and Bridy waiting for them. Police officers milled around, providing protection for the parents but also gravely concerned about their colleague. This was not what they had hoped to have happen but the reality of what the couple was facing made it almost impossible to have been avoided.

Toryn headed for the examination rooms and the emergency physician. He waited somewhat impatiently for the examinations to be completed before he approached.

"Doc? What can you tell me?" Toryn hesitated to ask.

"They've been drugged with something, Toryn. We're running blood panels now to determine what it was." The physician turned to Toryn, a hard look on his face. "I don't think it was anything illicit but we won't know for sure until we get the results back. Other than that, they're not harmed. But I understand where they were found. That is a rough area for wildlife."

"It is. They may not have survived an attack from a wild critter." Toryn looked around, seeing that officers had stationed themselves outside of the rooms.

"No, they not likely would have." The physician moved away, needing to look after other patients but nodding when Toryn asked if the parents could come back to the couple.

The parents were on their feet, heading for Toryn as he beckoned for them.

"Toryn?" Alin was almost afraid to ask about his son.

"They're alive, Alin, but they have been drugged. The physician is running drug panels to find out what it was but he didn't think that it was anything illegal." Toryn pointed behind him. "Come on back. It's okay to be with them."

Alin and Ardeen headed for Aidan as Bayne and Bridy headed for their daughter. Both sets of parents were grateful that their children were alive but they were still deeply worried about them. This was not how their day had been to go. All they could do was pray for God's protection on that day.

Toryn walked outside and found Lyle and George waiting for him. Andrew and Bill were there as well.

"Toryn? How are they?" Lyle spoke for the group.

"They're still unconscious. The physician said that they were drugged with something but they don't know what until the blood panels are back. He doesn't think it was street drugs." Toryn was troubled about that. "Their parents are with them."

Bill shared a look with Andrew. They had both patrolled the area when they were on the county force. Where they had found Aidan and Artis? That was a known area for wild animals. People had been attacked and even killed by coyotes and wolves in the area as well as wild dogs. That they found the couple was God working. They all acknowledged that.

"We have officers with them?" George looked around, feeling someone watching them but he could not pinpoint anyone that stood out.

"We do. The officers sorted it out themselves to work two hours shifts for both of them." Lyle sighed. "Where does the investigation stand, George"

"Not where it should be. That information that Aidan was handed has helped. I've been in contact with the investigator in Artis' home town. He has been doing what he can but he hasn't a clear picture of why."

"None of us seem to." Toryn was frustrated as were the others. "Andrew? What would you do?"

"What you are. Keep working it as you can. Talk to Aidan and Artis again and again. Talk to their friends, their parents. Sometimes all it takes is one conversation for someone to remember something." Andrew was not saying anything that the other officers had not one or were not aware of. He just didn't have any other words to tell them.

Toryn, Lyle, and George were nodding. They had done all that and would do it again and again. It didn't matter that Aidan was an officer and friend. They would do the same for anyone.

Alin watched his son carefully, not seeing any movement from him. His arm was around Ardeen as she sobbed softly. Neither one of them wanted this for their son. Only their wishes didn't seem to matter. God was in control, they had to admit.

———

Bayne had trouble controlling his anger at whoever it was who had harmed his daughter. He paced the examination room, his fists clenched. Bridy watched him and then their daughter. She too was angry but was praying it through even as she stood in that room. They didn't know who was after the couple. They only knew that someone had to be found and held responsible for the attacks.

"Bayne? What do we do? How do we help find the ones responsible?" Bridy turned back to him, finding him standing beside her.

"I don't know. I wish I knew who it was. I would go and find them and bring them to justice."

"It's not our place to do that, love. It's God's place to revenge. We need to pray for the investigators and a resolution to this. That's our part in this. That and to provide support for both Artis and Aidan and also his parents. Not to say the investigators."

Bayne sighed. He knew that Bridy was correct in her words. He prayed for God to forgive his anger even though he knew that God listened to all of his emotions and had been all of Bayne's life. He wasn't ashamed that at times, his emotions had gotten the best of him when he prayed.

Toryn stood for a moment, watching Alin and Ardeen and then Bayne and Bridy. He had no words of comfort to give to them. Everyone's emotions were raw. He turned with a frown on his face. He was being watched, he just didn't know who was the culprit.

Lyle approached him, handing over his phone. Toryn took it, a questioning look on his face. His face tightened when he read the message.

"You've traced it?"

"I have. The phone that sent it? It's here in the hospital. We just don't know who it belongs to. The name and address are false." Lyle was frustrated at that.

Chapter 26

Aidan began to stir early the next morning. His head tossed and turned as he moaned slightly. A hand rested on his forehead, stilling his motions for a moment before he began to toss his head again. Ardeen was unable to calm her son. She turned as she heard almost silent footsteps.

The nurse noted Aidan's motions and moved to do her check of his vitals. She frowned at Ardeen.

"He's waking up." Ardeen was hopeful that Aidan was going to be fine.

"It appears that he is. He'll continue to do so." The nurse studied Ardeen. "What can I get for you?"

"I'm fine. Thank you." Ardeen walked away at that, looking for Alin. She didn't find him. Instead she found George waiting for her. "George?"

"Ardeen? How is he?"

"He's waking up to some extent. You're here. You should be at home in your bed and asleep." Ardeen was exhausted from worry and lack of sleep.

George grinned at her, knowing how she was feeling.

"I know but I needed to be here for you. I also need to run something by you." George waited until Ardeen had seated herself. "I have been reading back through that paperwork. It doesn't make sense.

"No, it doesn't. I don't know that it was meant to. I think that it was a red herring, meant to throw us off." Ardeen had spent a lot of time pondering this.

"I suspect that you are correct. We have not been able to make any sense of what it was. The lab techs are going over it all but aren't finding anything." George yawned, not meaning to. His eyes closed and he slept, not meaning to but unable to stay awake.

Ardeen studied him and then the officers who were stationed in the waiting room and outside the rooms where she would find Aidan and Artis. She was worried about the couple and didn't know how to proceed. What George had told her had been no surprise. The two sets of parents had talked over the evening and had come to the conclusion that the information was not helpful at all.

Alin approached Ardeen, wrapping an arm around his wife of many years. She turned into his shoulder, tears shaking her for a moment. He looked up as Bayne and Bridy joined them.

"Bridy? Bayne? I thought that you two had gone home." Alin knew that he had done the same but had returned to be with his wife and son.

"We can't stay away. Not while our children are here." Bayne's eyes closed for a moment against his emotions.

"Like us. How is Artis?" Alin looked between the other couple.

"She's not rousing. They thought that she would have." Bridy was worried about her daughter.

"She's given up." Bayne was guessing at what the problem was.

"She could be. It might take Aidan being with her to waken her." Ardeen was searching for a way to end this. "We need to find out who is involved. I just don't that we can."

Bayne was nodding, his eyes on Bridy. They were trying to solve it themselves, but they didn't have the resources that were needed.

Aidan's eyes flew open and he jerked upright, searching the room. Artis was not there. Fear rose in him that she had disappeared or was dead. Pulling the intravenous line from his hand, he was on his feet, unsteady as that was, and reaching for his clothes to dress. Aidan paused to pray for his lady and then for the investigation. What had happened to them the day before had been not quite unexpected but he had prayed that something like that would not have happened.

Pausing just outside of the door, Aidan nodded at the officer on duty before he looked around. Spying another officer outside another door, Aidan hesitated.

"Artis is there, Aidan." The officer spoke quietly from beside him.

"I gathered that. I'll head that way. I just don't feel that steady." Aidan's hand was out against the wall to balance himself.

"Here. Let me help you." The officer's hand was out to grasp Aidan's upper arm as he turned away from his hospital room and towards Artis.

Aidan walked carefully towards the bed, reaching for the rail at the side of it. A hand came out to rest against Artis' face. She turned into it, a soft sigh coming from her. Aidan looked around and then just climbed up beside her and wrapped her tight to him. He slept, content that he was with his love and that they were safe for the moment.

The nurse paused as the officer at the door stopped her

"Aidan's in there." He nodded at the door.

"He is? I wasn't aware of that. Okay." The nurse walked into the room and paused, a smile crossing her face. She went about her duties before she stood and studied the couple. Aidan had been a friend since primary school days. She didn't know Artis but wanted to meet her and get to know her as a friend as well. She sighed and then walked away. Other duties were calling her

Lyle walked quietly through the hospital hallway, pausing as he spotted the two sets of parents in the waiting room and then George heading his way.

"George?" Lyle was puzzled. George was off duty and shouldn't be here.

"I had to come, Lyle. I know. I know. I'm off duty."

"I see. Did they say anything?" Lyle nodded towards the waiting room.

"Ardeen thinks the paperwork and photos are a red herring. I am inclined to agree with her. We haven't found anything in them that would explain anything." George let his frustration show.

"I have to agree with you, George. I too think that it was to send us off on a tangent. I wonder how much it played in yesterday. They headed towards Greenton because of it."

"And whoever sent the paperwork and photos were waiting for that." George rubbed at his face. "Where do we go from here?" He watched as Lyle simply shrugged.

Chapter 27

Aidan watched Artis closely later that afternoon. They had been discharged and sent home. The consensus was that they had been given a sedative of some sort. Neither one could remember what had happened and that distressed Artis to no end. They had just looked at one another, not sure what to say but trusting God to protect them. Artis had stated that God was looking out for them and that they had to trust Him. He wanted only good for them and not evil.

Walking away from Aidan, Artis headed for a shower and then clean clothes. She had refused the offers of help that had come her way. She was terrified of harm coming to anyone who helped them. That had been a threat that had been driven into her when they had been forced from the truck and then forced to drink from the bottles of water. Artis could remember that much. Aidan couldn't remember anything other than leaving their home that Saturday morning. He wished that he did so that Artis didn't bear the burden on her own.

Neither one could remember what the men looked like. They could remember that there had been four men and Artis had been adamant that there had been a female present. George had nodded as he had taken their statements. That was what they were hearing on the streets, that a female was involved.

Aidan's head drop as Artis walked away from him. He had expected her to react that way. He headed for a shower himself, knowing that he needed some time to think and try to come up with a plan to protect the love of his life. Every plan that he had come up with and attempted didn't seem to be working out so well. Aidan was getting desperate to find some way to do that.

Artis walked back through the house, looking for Aidan. She found him stretched out on their bed, sound asleep. Artis' hand rested on Aidan's cheek before she walked away. She too was praying for a plan that would work. She just didn't have that plan or knew who would have a plan. She and Aidan had talked it over so many times that she had lost track of what plans they had come up with and then discarded.

On his feet in the middle of the night, Aidan searched through his home. Something was off and he didn't know what. He pulled up the security feed and searched through it. He sighed. His feeling was that Artis and he had been taken out of the way for some reason. And the men around their home seemed to be that reason.

Artis roused as she realized that Aidan was not with her. She was on her feet and looking for him. A hand rested on his shoulder before his arm was around.

"What did you find?" Artis stared at the video that was still playing. "There are men around our home."

"They are. I think that we were taken out so that they could plant something outside." Aidan was on his feet, heading for the bedroom and tugging Artis with him. "Get dressed, sweetheart. We need to leave."

George walked towards where Aidan stood outside of his truck, the window rolled down so that Aidan and Artis could speak with one another. He had received the video feed that Aidan had sent to him and had found a crime scene team to head towards Aidan's home.

"Aidan?" George was somewhat shocked at the grim look on Aidan's face.

"We were taken out, George, so that they could work around our house without us knowing it. I want to know what they planted. And they planted something. That is obvious from their movements." Aidan was angry. His words were spat out.

George walked towards the head crime scene tech who had waved at him. He noted that all the team members had stepped back. He frowned, not understanding why.

"George? We need the bomb squad. There are explosives around the house. That's what they were doing." Wayne was livid with anger. Aidan was one of the detectives who always worked well with the team, not taking over but letting them do what they needed to and aiding as he could.

"That's what we were thinking. I asked Phil and his team to head this way. He should be here soon." George angled his body to study Aidan and then Artis. "I just want to know why."

"So do we. This with Aidan? It doesn't make sense. He doesn't have any enemies that we know of. I don't know Artis but she doesn't strike me as having enemies in her personal life."

George waited patiently for Wayne to continue. He knew that the other man had not said what he did without having thought through it all.

"What are your thoughts, Wayne?" George finally asked.

"What if it isn't directly Aidan or Artis? What if it is directed at someone else or even at the department? We've seen that before." Wayne looked over at Aidan. "Is that even possible?"

"It is. It's a thought that Lyle and I had just discussed." George waited once more. "Who do you think it's directed to?"

George paled as he heard who Wayne suggested. His hand was on Wayne's arm, pulling him away from the house.

"Why her?"

"She's prominent in town. She works with the force. I know that Aidan was involved in that investigation involving her mother. It just makes sense."

George had his phone out, calling Lyle.

"Lyle? Yeah, there are explosives around the house. Phil is here with his team. But Wayne had a thought. What if it's not Aidan or Artis that are the real targets?" George listened as Lyle muttered to himself. "He suggested someone. This is who." George heard the silence on the other end of the call as Lyle digested what he had said.

"Her? Yes, that could be it. Work on that angle, George." Lyle pocketed his phone. He was at the station and knew that Toryn had shown up. He went looking for him.

Toryn looked around from the file that he was studying as he waited for an officer to return to his desk. He walked towards Lyle, frowning at the look on his face.

"Lyle? George did call earlier. What did they find?"

"Explosives. We think that's why Aidan and Artis were got out of the way to do this. But Wayne asked George if Aidan was the true target. He suggested someone else." Lyle gave the name.

Toryn stared past Lyle, thinking through what George and Wayne had asked. This may be what is going on but he didn't know the connection between Aidan and that person.

"What's the connection between the two?"

"I have no idea. George will speak with Aidan and see what he knows. We'll start an investigation as well. George will finish up at Aidan's and then head here. I am afraid for Aidan and Artis and their parents. This is not how it was to go."

Chapter 28

Alin and Bayne tracked the couple down that morning, their faces concerned about them. Ardeen and Bridy were at a meeting at the church and would appear later.

Aidan turned to face his father and Bayne. He was still somewhat unsteady on his feet still. He was warned that it might be a few days before the sedative was out of his system. Aidan had pushed for more information and had been bluntly told that they had almost overdosed on the medication.

"Aidan? What happened earlier?" Bayne watched the younger man closer.

"Someone took us out and then used that time to plant explosives around the house." Aidan was angry at that. He was struggling to release that anger to God. He knew that Artis was having the same difficulty.

"They did what?" Alin's words exploded from him. This had not been what he had expected to hear. "Who?"

"We don't know. George has some thoughts that he's working through. He'll talk to us about what he's found when he can." Aidan leaned back against the kitchen counter, crossing his arms over his chest.

"What can we do, son?"Alin frowned at Aidan. "Has Emma come through with anything?"

"Not yet. She's been pulled into some investigations that can't wait. But she did say that

Darcy had some profiles for us and that Darcy and Doug would head our way in the next couple of days." It had not been what he had wanted to hear. Yet there was nothing he could do about it.

"I see. Emma would have one of her staff working it, knowing Emma. And one of them will be in touch." Alin shifted on his feet, turning to Bayne. "Bayne? You have thoughts?"

"I do. Aidan, I need to say something but I'm not sure how to say it. We've been looking at our families and the people involved. A lady named Kataleen has been in touch, just to work with us on family trees. I understand that her husband works for Abe. We were talking with her on Saturday. The questions that she asked have brought up memories that we buried, Bridy and me. We can't confirm the information now as the people who told it to us have passed on. However, the gist of it is that someone from our town moved here years ago and then moved on to Riverville. Relatives of hers are spread out throughout the region. George said that he would work on tracking them down." Bayne was becoming increasingly worried about his daughter and her groom..

"That's what I found out, Dad, Bayne." Aidan looked up to fix his eyes on his father's face. "I just wish this was over. We really don't have a sense of why."

"We know that, Aidan." Bayne just bowed his head and prayed for the couple. He felt an arm link with his and knew that it was Artis.

"Dad?" Artis spoke when Bayne had finished his prayer. "What are your thoughts?"

"My thoughts?" Bayne waited for his daughter to speak, knowing that she was trying to find the words to ask what she needed to ask.

"Yes, your thoughts. I want to know what you think about what happened. I know what I think and what Aidan thinks. George has spoken with us but not you or Alin."

"We have been discussing it, love." Bayne reached an arm around his daughter, his eyes on her face. "How be we find some coffee and then find seats in the office? We will likely need that computer of Aidan's. I did call a friend from Mistletoe who is an investigator. He is willing to meet with us. In fact, he suggested Wednesday night." Bayne moved his daughter towards the office.

"Samuel? And that means Blackie. What about Simon? Did you ask him too?" Artis smirked at her father and saw his answering grin. "What did he say?"

"Who are these people?" Aidan sat beside Artis, a questioning look on his face.

"Samuel is a private investigator and a good friend. We have shared many an hour in Bible study and prayer over the years. Blackie or Levi is his son. He was in the armed forces and when he retired, he went into partnership with his father. Simon is a friend of Blackie and in fact was in the same unit as Blackie. They will work what they can and then reach out to us. Wednesday was only a suggestion." Bayne looked at his son-in-law, seeing him nodding.

"That works. Mistletoe is not that far from here. I would be interested in hearing what they have to say. In the meantime, I want to do some research. I'm not allowed to return to work this week, just to let the sedative fully leave my system. Artis and I have already put some thoughts down. I would be interested in hearing what you and Dad think."

Alin reached for the binder that he had dropped onto Aidan's desk. He and Bayne had been working together over the last few days and had sorted out into sections what they had found. They had not liked their findings at all.

"Here, son. This is what we have come up with. I can tell you that I'm not comfortable with our findings." Alin's face was sober before he searched the room, taking in the light green walls, the book shelves and pictures and mementos on the walls that meant a lot to Aidan. He smiled as he saw that Artis had been adding and rearranging the wall decor.

"I see." Aidan shared a look with Artis who nodded. "Can we pray first, Dad? I know that you two would have bathed this in prayer but I just fear for everyone involved. I feel danger approaching at a rapid pace. We just can't take any chances though. I also know that we can't protect ourselves properly if we don't know who are enemies are."

"You are correct in those words, son." Alin had been praying hourly for the couple. "Let's do that now and then we'll go over what we've found. And both of your moms have been involved. They would not do anything else."

Artis grinned for a moment, knowing that Alin had given a clear picture of the mothers.

"They wouldn't let you do anything without their input. We need that." Artis opened the binder and began to read. She was on her feet within minutes and reached for pads of paper and pens for both herself and Aidan.

Aidan took his with a quiet word of thanks, feeling Artis leaning against him as they read the material and made their notes. They shared a look when they finished.

"Dad? You have found a lot." Aidan was impressed but not surprised.

"We have, son. We have passed it on to Emma who will verify what we found. She will then pass it on to George. We chose to go that route as we wanted someone independent to your force to look it over. Emma said that she would provide it to Abe's team and that a friend of theirs who is a detective will take a look at it. It will not be set aside." Alin turned as he heard footsteps and the two mothers appeared.

"I see. We need to verify it all. I can do that but it would not be proper and correct." Aidan sat back, lost in thought. He felt Artis' hand on his and turned to her. "Artis?"

"We need a plan to catch this person. George will work through it in a proper manner, won't he, and then obtain the proper warrants. We can come up with a plan to trap the ones involved. This had taken over our lives and I want it to end. Every one of us does. Now, how do we do this?"

Ardeen sat close to her son, a thought crossing her mind. She nodded as the thought gelled. She spoke quietly, seeing the shock that her words elicited and then the determination to prove them correct.

Chapter 29

Artis walked through their backyard the next morning. Aidan had been on a conference call and she was at loose ends. She studied the gardens but decided that they didn't need any work done in that today. Her thought turned to what Ardeen had told them about the day before.

Artis turned as she heard footsteps, reaching to hug Slaney. Slaney had made sure to keep in contact over the last few days. Artis was glad for that. She had spent hours talking with Slaney, just getting her story and her thoughts on what Aidan and Artis were going through.

"Slaney? I was not expecting to see you today." Artis reached to hug her friend.

"I had to come, Artis. God told me that I had to." She looked around, not feeling anything off that day. "I don't feel anything here today."

"No, I don't either. It is a relief, to tell you the truth." Artis pointed to the back of the yard. "Let's sit back there. It's shaded to some extent. The sun is warm today, not what I expected from the weather report."

"It's a beautiful day. Now, talk to me. Tell me what news you have." Slaney waved her phone. "I'll take notes that we can share with the other ladies. And we are meeting for prayer and Bible study this afternoon at my place. We want you there."

"You do? That sounds so wonderful. I haven't had that before." She watched as Aidan headed their way, a tray in his hands. "Aidan?"

"I'm not staying. Here. I bought you ladies some sustenance." He dropped a kiss on Artis' cheek before he walked away.

Artis stared after him, a hand on her cheek. He was doing that more often, she decided, and she didn't mind one bit. She had fallen in love with her groom and from his actions, knew that he was in love with her. They would need to talk at some point.

Slaney turned to Artis and studied her. She nodded. Toryn was correct.

"Artis? What happened yesterday?"

Artis shook for a moment, her emotions raw.

"Ardeen had an idea of who it is that is after us and why. It makes sick sense." Artis mentioned the name, seeing Slaney draw in a sharp breath. "Slaney?"

"Her?" Slaney continued to stare at Artis. "You wouldn't know her. Anyone from this town would." She pulled up some information on her phone and then handed the phone to Artis. "This is who she is and what she is supposed to do. She flies under the radar, as they say. The authorities have been trying to find the information that they need to arrest her."

"And we just had to be the ones God chose to bring her to justice." Artis settled back against the bench. "We need to make plans, Slaney. When we meet this afternoon, can we do that?"

"We can. We'll do a potluck for supper and our guys will be there and ready to help sort all this out." Slaney reached for Artis' hand and pulled her to her feet. "Come on, friend. Let's find something in your kitchen to prepare for tonight." Slaney grinned at Artis who beamed back at her. They rushed towards the house, startling Aidan.

"Ladies?" Aidan reached to hug Artis.

"I'm heading to Slaney's for a meeting with the ladies for prayer and Bible study. Then, we're meeting with all the guys tonight. And that means you." Artis was grinning at her groom, her beauty taking his breath away for a moment. All he could do was reach to kiss her.

"All right then. Have a wonderful afternoon." Aidan walked away, glad that Slaney had shown up and involved Artis with the ladies who were married to his friends.

Slaney pointed to the fridge in her kitchen, opening the door for Artis to tuck away the salad that she had prepared.

"That looks so good. Thank you, Artis, for coming. It's not easy being the new girl on the block. I'm the last one to join this group and they have all welcomed me." She grinned at her friends. "We'll spend our time in prayer and Bible study and then start on our research. We've done this before for everyone."

"You have? That's what I was told that Richard's team did."

"That they did. Have you met Emma yet?"

"Yes. She's working on this as well as much as she can. She has a friend who is heading our way with a profile."

"Darcy. And her husband, Doug, will be with her. He's the lead on Riverville's ETF." Slaney handed over a bottle of water as she heard the front door open.

The ladies had welcomed Artis in a way that she had not expected. She had had to blink back tears as she listened to their prayers. The study of Christ's prayer in the garden was just what she had needed. The reminder that she had been prayed for all those years ago by her Saviour was the breath of fresh air in her adventure that was required and so welcome.

With the men milling around with their ladies, Toryn felt that his house was almost too full but he also knew that both Aidan and Artis needed this time. Slaney had approached him when he entered the house, walking into his hug. He could feel her emotions simmering just under the surface.

"Slaney?" His voice was kept low.

"It's heartbreaking, Toryn. She didn't have many friends, Artis confessed to us. She is unsure if she should be around us, thinking that she'll bring us danger."

Toryn stared at Artis as she stood with Aidan's arm around her. He could see Aidan speaking with her but Artis didn't seem to be responding.

"It's all new for her, that's a given." Toryn stood for a moment. He had had a chance to speak with George and had not been surprised at the turn that the investigation had taken.

Aidan looked around at Toryn at that moment, a frown on his face. Toryn had dropped to see Aidan just after the ladies had left. He had spent time in prayer with his friend and then bluntly asked him what his thoughts were. Aidan had not been surprised at that. He had handed him his notes. Toryn had not been surprised at that. He had then taken time to pray with Aidan.

Chapter 30

A week later, Artis rose from where she had been sitting at the desk. Aidan was back to work and she was bored. Squinting at the clock, Artis sighed. It would soon be time for their dinner and she had no desire to cook that day.

Hearing the door bell, Artis frowned. They were not expecting anyone that day, not that she was aware. She peeked through the door window, staring at the police shield that the man was holding.

"Can I help you?" Artis had opened the door but blocked it in such a way that she could slam it shut quickly.

"You must be Artis. I'm Darcy Foster and this is my husband, Doug. Slaney said that she had mentioned we might head this way soon."

"She did. I'm sorry. Come on it." Artis stood back from the door, accepting the hug from Darcy and then Doug. "I was just heading for the kitchen." Artis bit at her lip, knowing that she had to prepare a meal but not sure what to serve.

"It's okay, Artis." Darcy knew how she felt to some extent. "We picked up some subs and salads for a meal. We don't show up at mealtime without bringing something."

"Thank you. I was working away and lost track of time." Artis blinked back tears, not wanting to cry in front of them. She felt arms around her and leaned back against Aidan. "Aidan? You're home."

"I am. And Doug and Darcy are here." He reached to shake their hands, not willing to let go of his lady.

"They brought a meal for us." Artis was distraught at that thought.

"It's okay, sweetheart. It's what we do with our friends. I've done the same." Aidan moved away from Artis, reaching for dishes. Artis moved to help him.

Doug sat back at last, wiping his hands on a napkin. His keen eyes were assessing both Aidan and Artis. They were stressed, he could tell, but also determined to solve their adventure.

"Aidan? What can you tell us?" Doug reached for the pad of paper and pen that Darcy handed to him.

"Not a lot. We have a suspicion of who it might be but nothing proven." Aidan explained what they had discovered and what they thought. "Dad has spoken to some friends who are investigators and they are hoping to have some information confirmed this week."

"And you are afraid to go out and about? We have heard about that. You know our story. Artis, what can we do for you?"

Artis shrugged. She was not used to being asked what someone could do for her. She had been independent all her life and that was changing now that she had Aidan in her life.

"I'm not sure. What can you tell us? Darcy? Slaney said that you did profiles."

"I do. And I have done one for you and Aidan. George has a copy, but this is yours. It sounds as if you are working through the profile without having seen it." Darcy grinned at her. "In a nutshell? The woman you describe is who I would profile. There are others involved though. You need to be on your guard even here at home. They will not hesitate to kidnap you again. As to which one of you is the target? I didn't get a sense that it was truly one of you. You are being used to get to someone else. I am still working on that."

"If it's not us, then why? Why try and kill Aidan? Why plant explosives around our home? Why sedate us as they did? It doesn't make a lot of sense." Artis shared a look with Aidan. "We thought at first it was because of me and one of the youths that I worked with. Or one of their families. That doesn't seem plausible now. Aidan? It's possible that it was someone that he had met on an investigation."

"It's possible that could be it." Doug shared a look with Aidan. They both had been around the block a time or two as was the common phrase. They had seen too much and that affected how they looked at life. "And it could be something totally different. That's what Darcy is picking up on. She's the best that I have ever seen in providing profiles for people that she has never met. That's what she used to do until she was treated wrongly by a former police chief. And she is even better when she has met the person." Doug shared a look with Darcy. "She'll refine the profile now that she has met you."

"That I will, Artis. But for now, show us your information. We have time to go over it with you." Darcy and Doug had been prepared to spend the night in Oak City if necessary.

Aidan was on his feet and to his office, returning with the folders that Artis had organized that day for them. He handed them to Doug who nodded. Doug appreciated the fact that they were organized. This would help them as they went through them.

Darcy took the folders as Doug finished with them. Reading through them, she reached for the pad of paper and pen that sat on the table beside Doug. She rapidly made her own notes, pausing frequently to digest something that she had read. Artis watched her, fascinated with how Darcy was reacting to the information.

"Darcy?" Artis finally had to ask her new friend what she thought. "What are you thinking? And I know that you have found something in all that information."

"I have. I just need to think a bit more." Darcy sat back, staring across the kitchen. She finally looked at Doug who was watching her intently. He nodded. They had both found the same information and person, he knew.

"Aidan. Artis. The supposition that this is not about you is partly correct. There is someone who is after you and means your deaths. Somehow you two are connected. It is likely through your work. Have you two ever met before? Is there someone in common that you have dealt with that you didn't know about?"

Aidan and Artis shared a look. That was not something that they had considered to any degree. Aidan was now at a loss as to how to proceed. The information that they needed was not readily available due to confidentiality restrictions.

"That is possible, Doug. I just don't know how we would ever prove it. Without a name and confirmed evidence to go forward with that, we can't go forward with that." Aidan was frustrated at that. If this would mean the end of their adventure, he wanted to do that. He felt Artis' hand on his and he laid his other one on top of hers.

Chapter 31

Aidan walked away after closing the door behind Doug and Darcy. He appreciated their coming to speak with them and leaving the profiles behind for Aidan and Artis. He was just frustrated because they didn't seem to be much further along in the investigation. Aidan had received a text message from George, asking that he could meet with both he and Artis in the morning. Aidan had agreed, knowing that George might have some information that would bring comfort to Artis.

Artis was waiting for him, walking into his hug and just holding on. She didn't speak for a moment and then leaned back to look up at him.

"Aidan? Did we accomplish anything?"

"I think so. Darcy would not have given us the profile unless she was certain about it. And Dad has heard back from Samuel. They want to meet with us tomorrow night if we can." He looked down at her, seeing the troubled look in her eye. "We need to talk at some point, Artis, about where we go as a couple. I just want you to know that I love you deeply and don't want to lose you. I want to spend the rest of our lives together, if God so wills."

"You do?" Artis stared in wonder at him. "I love you too, Aidan. God brought us together. I have listened to the other ladies' stories. Ours sounds like theirs but we are all unique in what we are facing and who we are facing. I am afraid for you when you're on the job. I know that I can't be there with you. All I can do is to pray that God protects you."

Aidan bent to kiss her and then simply held her. His emotions were in a turmoil, almost a whirlpool, he thought. He was afraid for Artis as well, not being able to be with her all the time.

"What do we do?" Artis laid her head against Aidan. "I'm afraid for you and for me. And I am also afraid for our parents. Will they go after them?"

"I am not sure, Artis. That is always a possibility. They are watching us closely, that much I know. We're not receiving the letters and packages that others have. The ones that we have received? They don't make much sense in the investigation."

"Someone was trying to throw us off. That's what those were meant for. I know that there was a code deciphered but it didn't seem to make much sense." Artis chewed at her lip, studying the living room as she did so. She liked how Aidan had done with it and would not want to change anything about it.

"That's what George has decided. He and Lyle discussed it in detail." Aidan turned Artis to the living room and to a sitting position on the couch. "We need to look past that and determine what we have. George can't tell us everything."

Artis snuggled close to Aidan, her thoughts troubled.

"What is God teaching us in all of this? The ladies said that He had a teaching for each of them."

"What is He teaching us?" Aidan thought for a moment. "That's a good question. That's one that we can ask Gideon." Gideon was their minister and a good friend of Aidan'.

"We can but what can we determine ourselves? I think that He is teaching us to trust Him more. He is there for us at all times, never leaving us. He hides us in the hollow of His hand. Even when bad things happen, He is in the midst of the storm and calms the winds around us. Sometimes He calms us instead. I think of this as being in a tornado. Right now, we're in the centre of it and it's calm. We're coming to the edge of it again and that means a lot of danger for us."

"That is well put, sweetheart. We are in the middle of a storm and we are approaching a dangerous time. We have to trust, no matter how hard it seems to be." He dropped a kiss on the top of her head. "I hate that you are going through this. But if you hadn't been at that diner, I would not have met the helpmeet that God had prepared for me."

"I like how you think, buster." Artis grinned at him for a moment before she sobered. "I want this over, Aidan, and over now. Do you think that it will be?"

"It will be soon. I sense that with what we have now and what Emma is sending to George, we will be close to ending this. I just pray that we are not hurt more than we have been."

Artis thought through the profile that Darcy had left for her. Something about the person seemed familiar but she wasn't sure. She turned to look at

Aidan, finding that he had dozed off. She sighed. Her wish had been to speak with him would have to be set aside for the present. Artis snuggled down against Aidan and reached for her phone. A smile crossed her face as she read through the messages that were waiting for her. A question from Daci had her pausing to think about her answer.

Daci had asked Artis when she was in Oak City last. Artis nodded. She had been in Oak City for a conference at the church a year ago. It had been for young adults. Artis frowned and looked up at Aidan. Had he been there? Had they connected somehow without her remembering him? Images nudged at the end of her mind and she sighed. They had been in a workshop together and had sat almost side by side. She had forgotten that. Now, Artis needed to talk it over with Aidan. That would have to wait until later.

On her feet, Artis paced the hallway in the house, not wanting to leave but not wanting to stay. Her emotions were in a turmoil. And she just didn't know how to react to what was being discovered. Artis moved to where she could watch Aidan. She wanted to talk to him but she didn't want to waken him.

Aidan stirred briefly, his eyes flickering open before he slept again. He snuggled down under the blanket that Artis had covered him with. She had stood when she finished with her hand on his head.

A noise from the outside had Artis jumping before she crept to the window, peeking around the curtains. She didn't see anything but she was certain that someone had been around the house. She froze as she saw the flickering light moving back across the front yard. She let the curtain drop back into place and almost ran to sit beside Aidan before she snuggled up close to him under the blanket. Aidan made her feel safe, even when he was asleep.

Neither one of the couple roused overnight. In the early morning light, Aidan was awake, watching Artis before he scooped her into his arms and tucked her into their bed. He walked back through to the kitchen, a frown on his face. Aidan was disturbed and not sure why.

———

Chapter 32

Monday morning found George staring at the report in his hands before he was on his feet. Lyle needed to see this before he spoke with Aidan. And he would be speaking with Aidan. This person who was named was close to Aidan. George just didn't see how he fit into the picture.

Lyle looked around as George tracked him down in one of the conference rooms. He frowned at George before he took the papers that George kept thrusting towards him.

"What is this?" Lyle was puzzled at the look on George's face.

"This person? He's close to Aidan. We received word from another police force that he's looking for Aidan and not for Aidan's health. That person has been involved in crime, including murder." George was anxious to say the least.

Lyle's frown deepened before he began to read the paperwork, flipping through it more than once.

"It's all verified, George. Where is Aidan this morning?" Lyle walked from the room, intent on finding Aidan.

"He's out on the streets on a case. In the downtown area. A robbery and murder from early this morning." George reached for his jacket and then his car keys. "I'm heading that way to find him."

"Send a car to his home to watch out for Artis. That is, if she's home." Lyle was frustrated with Artis. She just came and went as she willed, going about her daily tasks. She had glared at him when he asked that she have someone with her when she did so. Her comment was that she never knew when she wanted to go out somewhere and that she was certainly not waiting for an escort. He could think again if he thought that. Lyle had bitten back a smile at her look. She was exactly who Aidan needed in his life.

"I have done that. They said her car is there but they didn't go up to the house." George walked away, heading for his car and then to find Aidan. He found the other detective standing at his car, his note book out on the trunk as he made notes. He simply stopped beside Aidan and waited.

Aidan glanced at him for a moment before he went back to his notes. He sighed. George had not found him just because. Something had come up. He prayed that it was about another case but he had his doubts on that. Tucking away his note book into a pocket, Aidan took a moment to pray before he looked at George.

"George?"

"Where can we talk, Aidan? I need to go over a report with you. And yes, it concerns you and Artis."

Aidan pointed towards a nearby cafe.

"In there. I could use a coffee about now." Aidan waited for their coffees to be set down on the red laminate tabletop and the server to move away before he looked up at George. "Okay, George. I know it's not good news. I can tell by the look on your face."

"It's not. I don't know quite how to say this."

"Spit it out. It can't be any worse than it already is." Aidan frowned at the look on George's face. "As long as Artis and our parents are fine, then I can handle it."

"As far as I know, they are fine. An officer is parked outside of your home as we speak." George swallowed hard, trying to sort out his thoughts. "How close are you to Ted Lang?"

"Ted? Not that close. We were in classes together at high school. I see him once in a while and just chat about general things. Why?" Aidan kept his eyes fastened on George. "How is he involved?"

"We just received word that he could be. A police detective from across the province arrested him for robbery and murder. He found some evidence in Lang's belongings suggesting that he was after you." George watched as Aidan absorbed his words before he spoke again. "Again, Aidan, how close was he to you?"

Aidan shrugged. He had not seen Lang in at least six months and then that was only to say hello in passing. Neither man had taken time to talk.

"I haven't seen him in at least six months. And then we only said hello. I know that his parents and siblings all left town ten years ago. It was odd that Lang kept coming back but he does have relatives here and also some friends. He was never a real friendly guy to get to know. He kept a lot to himself."

"I see. I told Lyle that I would speak with you. You grew up in this town, Aidan. I didn't. I need you to give me a list of his friends and relatives. He had it in for you for some reason. We need to find out why and if he's the one behind it."

Aidan was shaking his head.

"He's not. He's related to that woman. A great-nephew if I am remembering correctly on his father's side. I'll get a list to you of all of those people once I'm back in the office." Aidan rubbed absentmindedly at his mug. "Artis is really hurting, George, and I don't know how to help her. She's talking with the ladies but still doesn't want to burden them too much if she can help it."

"That's her character, Aidan. She doesn't want to be a burden. She's seen too much during her time as a youth protection worker. That has to hurt to see kids going through hard times."

"It does. She's beginning to open up some about her time working there. Neither of us can get a sense that this is related to that although there might be a connection."

"I don't know that there is." George tilted his mug to study the coffee in it. "It's related to here, Aidan. We're not getting a sense that it's you directly but something along the lines of what we talked about. I know your history and who you are connected to. Could this be related to your uncle who died so young?"

Aidan nodded. He had had a long talk with his father the day before. His uncle Aaron had been killed in a robbery gone wrong when Aidan was a young teen. That killing had never been solved.

"Uncle Aaron. He was killed in a robbery at the jewelry store he owned and that killing is still on the books as an open case. I know the cold case detectives look at it every year. There is just something missing that would solve it." Aidan was sober as he spoke. He knew that his father missed his older brother a lot. Aidan wanted to solve the filling and bring closure to his family. He had just never found that one piece that was needed.

Chapter 33

Aidan laid the list of names on George's desk and then walked back through the police building to the back parking lot. He paused for a moment, his keys in his hand, as he stared up at the sky. It was growing late in the season and the days were not as long as they had been. Aidan sighed. He wanted to take Artis out for a meal that night but his conversation with George was still troubling him.

Artis turned as she heard the front door open and then close and then the sound of the closet door closing. Aidan was home and she had no meal ready for him. Her thoughts had been especially troublesome that day and she had spent the afternoon bowed before her Heavenly Father, ignoring any calls or text messages that had come through.

Aidan studied his bride and then simply held out his arms. Artis almost threw herself at him.

"You okay, sweetheart?" Aidan's voice was muffled as his head was bent over her hair.

"No, I'm not. I'm so afraid, Aidan, and I don't know why." Artis struggled to control her sobs, not wanting to burden him.

"It's okay, sweetheart. Cry if you need to. But that's not all."

"No, it's not. I'm just so worried about our parents. They could be harmed or killed because of this. And we still have no reason as to why."

Aidan drew her into the kitchen and shoved her into a chair. He reached for bottles of water from the fridge and handed one to her before he sat beside her. His arm was around her as he prayed for her.

"Artis, George received word this morning that an acquaintance of mine was arrested on the other side of the province. He had documentation that threatened me. As we were talking, I mentioned that Dad's oldest brother had been killed during a robbery at his jewelry store. That has never been solved. He's looking into that. And the person who was arrested? He's a great-nephew to the female we think is behind this."

Artis studied him before she just hugged him. She could sense the feeling of sorrow and pain that he felt.

"And you think the two are related somehow?"

"I do. Lang never seemed to be a troublemaker when we were in school but it can be hidden."

"Lang?" Artis paled at that. "What's his first name?" When she heard it, her head dropped onto her folded arms. "I know him, Aidan. Please, God, not him."

Aidan was dumbstruck at her words and just wrapped an arm around her. His head was touching hers as he prayed for the love of his life.

"Artis? How do you know him?"

Artis looked up, a bleak look on her face, the tears still fresh on her cheeks.

"He threatened me a year or less ago. I had witnessed a robbery in a local shop. He was there. He wasn't one of the robbers but I always wondered if he was connected to them. The detective warned me about him. Apparently they received a threat directed at me and signed by him. Who does that?"

"Either someone really stupid or someone trying to frame him. Do you remember the name of the detective?" Aidan's phone was out as he sent the information on to George.

George stared at the text message before he shook his head. These two were connected in ways that no one seemed to recognize. He wondered if that information would have ever come out if Aidan and Artis had never met. He headed for Lyle and then Toryn. This development was something that they could not just set aside.

Aidan rose and glanced at the clock. Artis would not want to be going out anywhere, he decided, and paused as he heard a tap at the front door. He walked that way, frowning at Ben as he opened the door.

"Here you go, Aidan. I just sensed that you two needed this tonight. No charge." Ben was gone before Aidan could respond.

Aidan set the food on the table and stared at Artis who stared at the bag.

"Ben?"

"Ben. He does this. He senses when people need something like this and reaches out." Aidan drew her to her feet. "It's not too cold out. Let's eat on the back deck."

———

Sitting back, their meal finished, Aidan prayed for words. He needed to talk to Artis but he wasn't sure how to broach what he needed to.

Artis studied her groom, sensing the unsettled emotions that he was struggling with.

"Aidan? Can we leave all this behind and run away for a couple of days?" Artis needed to get away, to clear her head, and find peace once more. That wasn't possible in this town.

Aidan looked up at her, surprise on his face at her request. He grinned.

"We can do that. We can run away. I have a couple of days of personal leave that I need to use. Lyle will let me take off Thursday and Friday. That will give up four days. Anywhere in particular?"

Artis started to shake her head before she frowned at him.

"Your dad's friend? The one from Mistletoe? Can we head to that town?"

"We can. In fact, they are having a harvest festival this weekend. I know that Blackie or Samuel would have a place for us to stay. If not, then one of their friends, Finn? Her parents have a bed and breakfast." Aidan's phone was out as he sent off a message to Mary, who responded that they didn't need to book a room. They would just use her father's old bedroom at no charge and she would be glad to see them.

Artis leaned against Aidan as she read the response and was surprised but not surprised. It was what she was coming to expect from Aidan's circle of friends.

"They would do that?"

"They would. It's not the first time that they have done this. It will do us good to get away." Aidan sent off a quick message to Lyle who responded promptly. He agreed with the time off but cautioned Aidan that he would need to update him on his investigations by Wednesday.

Chapter 34

Watching as Aidan drove into Mistletoe on the Thursday, Artis was enthralled by the town. It was the first town that had interested her in a long time, she thought.

"We need to come back at Christmas." Aidan grinned at her as she enthusiastically nodded. "I've been here then and it is something to see." He looked around for a parking spot, not finding one right away. "Samuel doesn't live too far from here. We could park there. Or here instead." Aidan took the empty parking spot, came around to grasp Artis' hand, and then locked the car. He sensed someone had followed them but he could not see anyone who stood out to him. It was just his years of experience that told him someone was watching them.

Artis stared around, not comfortable being out in the open and not in their town. She wasn't sure after all if this had been that good of an idea.

Three hours laters, Aidan grinned as he led her into a small cafe called The House. He knew the owner, a friend of Blackie's, and knew that the food would be excellent. Aidan stared at him and then around the cafe. There didn't see to be any empty spots and she sighed. She was starved, she decided, but it looked as if they would not be eating any time soon. She frowned at the young lady around her own age who approached Aidan, greeting him with a hug.

"Artis, this is a friend's wife, Leah Smithson. Josh owns this restaurant. Leah, this is my bride, Artis."

Leah looked at her and then reached to hug Artis.

"I often wondered what Aidan's lady would look like. You're perfect for him." Leah looked around and then pointed to a booth near the kitchen. "Come this way. I was working in that booth but you two need to use it. Josh will be out to greet you as soon as he knows that you're here. And I know that the others will be around." She frowned at Aidan. "You're on your own adventure, aren't you?"

"We are, Leah. And it's not over. Dad has reached out to Samuel, Blackie, and Simon."

"They mention that your father had contacted them, just not why. I know that they are very worried about you and Artis. What can we do to help?" Leah slid onto a booth seat, shifting her work to one side.

"For now? I really don't know. We'll run everything by you and see what ideas all of you have." Aidan looked up as a hand landed on his shoulder. "Josh?"

"Aidan. It's good to see you again. And this is Artis?" Josh grinned at them.

"That would be Artis." Aidan hesitated for a moment.

"We'll meet tonight, Aidan. Mary said that you were staying with them. We can meet there or at one of our places."

"How be we meet at Blackie's?" Aidan's attention was drawn to the man who had entered, his eyes on Aidan and then Artis. "Josh, do you know that man that just entered?"

Josh looked around, studying the older man.

"No, I can't say that I do. Is he following you?"

"He seems to be. I saw him in Oak City over the last couple of days. He seems to be following us." Aidan's hand reach for Artis. "I wonder who he is."

Josh snapped a photo of the man and forwarded it to both Blackie, who worked as a private investigator, and also to Simon, who had worked as a police officer before joining Samuel and Blackie as an investigator. He knew that they would search for any information for him.

"We'll see what the fellows can come up with." Josh walked away, intent on finding food for the couple.

Samuel looked around as Simon appeared in his doorway. He reached for the papers that Simon handed him.

"What's this?"

"Josh sent the photo. Aidan's in town and he was followed by this man. I know him. He's not someone who Aidan needs to have tailing him."

Samuel read through the material and nodded.

"We're meeting with them tonight." Simon walked away, intent on finding out as much as he could before their meeting.

Artis tugged Aidan with her as she walked through the town. She was happy and carefree for the moment. Aidan was on constant alert but also happy. He liked that Artis felt free enough to enjoy herself.

"Aidan? That man from the restaurant? Is he still following us?" Artis looked around for a moment.

"I don't think that he is. Josh said that he would try and keep him in the cafe. He has contacts with the police here who would move in and do that."

"I'm glad. I want to enjoy these few days but I'm still afraid."

"So am I, sweetheart. So am I." He pointed to a store. "This is Jacob's wife's store. Fynn inherited it from her grandfather. It has a lot of interesting antiques."

"Oh, that sounds wonderful." She paused as Aidan didn't move.

"Her mother is our hostess for the next few days. And yes, she and Jacob did have an adventure as did their four friends. I suspect the ladies will meet with us tonight." Aidan opened the door and waited for Artis to enter. He was disappointed that Fynn wasn't there but he knew that they would meet at some point.

Samuel watched Aidan as he followed Artis around the store. He had felt compelled to come and find him, knowing the character of the man who had followed him.

"Aidan?" Samuel stopped beside the younger man.

"Samuel? You're here? I don't like that you are." Aidan watched Artis closely, knowing that she had not alerted to Samuel being there.

"Aidan? We're meeting tonight. For now, I have a couple of my men here. They'll follow you and make sure that you're safe while you're in town. The man who you saw? He's a bit of a nasty character." Samuel walked away as Artis approached Aidan.

"Aidan?"

"That was Samuel, sweetheart. We have shadows while we're here. We won't see them, knowing Samuel's men, unless we need to." Aidan reached for the old teapot that Artis had in her hand. "I like this. It's perfect."

"It is." Artis paid for it and then took the bag that she was handed. "Where now?"

"How be we find our accommodations?" Aidan grinned at her before he hugged her.

Chapter 35

Blackie stood and watched the group that had gathered. He could hear Julia and Fynn behind him preparing the trays that held the food that had been prepared. He was worried about his friend and his lady. Blackie's mother and Fynn's mother had gladly taken the children for the evening.

Turning as he heard footsteps stopping beside him, Blackie studied his father. Samuel was upset, his son could tell.

"Dad?"

"It's not good, Blackie. I don't know how we'll protect them. Knowing Aidan, he won't hide."

"No, he won't." Blackie was watching Artis, finding her staring at him. "Artis won't either. So, how do we do this then, Dad?"

"I don't know, son. Let's eat and then spend some time in prayer. We'll discuss everything, make our suggestions, and then pass everything on to his supervisor."

The next morning found Aidan awake early. His arm was wrapped around Artis as she slept, his prayer rising for her and begging God for protection for her. He just wasn't sure how to proceed. And that was not him. He was usually focused and determined to follow the path that he had set before himself.

On his feet, Aidan dressed and then headed out for a run. He needed that. Josh had told him that he should be safe in the neighbourhood of the B&B. Aidan didn't plan on being out long but he did need his run.

Artis roused an hour later, not seeing Aidan in the room. She was on her feet as well, dressed and then headed downstairs. They had been told to make themselves at home. Artis knew that she and Aidan needed to discuss the information from the night before. They had agreed to set it aside until they went home, that was if they could. She had no doubt that they were being followed. And that disturbed Artis. She didn't like that feeling.

Fynn turned to welcome her and then frowned at her.

"I know you, Artis. I just don't know from where."

Artis shrugged. They had all said that the night before. She didn't see how and stated as much to Fynn.

"I have never been in this town, Fynn. I don't see how you would know me." She frowned at Fynn and shrugged.

"It's just that we think we know you. And for all of us to have that feeling is unusual." Fynn turned as Jacob and Aidan entered. "Jacob? Where would we know Artis from?"

"From that conference in her town a year or so ago. She spoke about how to prepare oneself to face difficulties in the type of work that she does."

Artis blinked and then frowned at him.

"I had forgotten about that. I really didn't want to speak but was talked into it." She shuddered. "I felt evil there that day and left as soon as I finished. I never did find out why." Artis looked at Aidan. "I'm sorry. I forgot about that."

"It's okay.   I think George mentioned it. Someone from your town had told him about it." Aidan's arm was around her. "The problem is that now we're getting too much information and will need to sort through it all to determine what is the correct info that we can work with. We'll do that once we get home. For the next three days, we're on vacation and aren't going to think about our adventure."

Artis snorted, bringing grins to the faces of the others.

"You might be able to do that. I can't do that." Artis smirked at Aidan. She turned away, a wink sent Fynn's way that had the other lady choking back laughter.

Heading for their home late on the Sunday afternoon, Artis' thoughts turned to their adventure as it was called. Samuel had approached them at church that morning and handed over a thick manilla envelope. He had shaken his head at their questioning look, simply telling them to read it over and then contact him if they had any questions. His look said that they would.

"Okay, sweetheart?" Aidan reached to lay a hand against her cheek, a soft smile on his face.

———

185

"I am, my love. I am." Artis smiled at him in return before her attention turned to the outside. Her thoughts were troubled.

"We'll look over that material. Thanks for running away with me for the last few days."

"We need this. We're refreshed in mind and spirit. They're a fun group of friends."

"They are. The guys all served in the same unit in the army and all ended up as descendants of the founding families of the town. And the four ladies are all related as well. It was quite an adventure they all had." Aidan slowed to make his turn into Oak City. He paused before he headed for a restaurant. "I know that we've eaten out for the last few days. Let me pick up something and then we can take it home."

Artis nodded, her thoughts troubled and dark. She had been thinking through all that they had gone through and it was disturbing. She knew that it was far from over.

"What is God teaching us, Aidan?"

"What is He teaching us?" He shot her a quick glance and saw her nod.

"Yes. What is He teaching us." Artis knew that there was a lesson in there somewhere. She just wasn't seeing it.

"He is teaching us. He is also protecting and defending us. He wants us to learn to trust in a new and deeper way. He wants only His best for us. We need to remember that we were prayed for in the Garden." Aidan paused before he continued, pulling into a parking spot at a restaurant as he did so. "He is teaching us that He is in control and that He has a plan for our lives. It's sometimes hard to see that but He is with us each moment of each day"

"I get that. It's sometimes hard to see that when we're going through things. How do people without faith do this?" Artis didn't expect an answer. She knew that Aidan understood her thoughts.

Aidan paused for a moment to pray for her lady. This was coming up to the most dangerous time, he knew. He didn't want any harm to come to the love of his life.

Chapter 36

Artis headed into the local library two days later. She needed to find something to do, she decided, and thought the library would be the place to do just that. She paused just inside the door and then turned and walked back out of the building. Artis just could not walk any further into it. Something stopped her, and she acknowledged that it was God. He had turned her away from that building for a reason.

Daci frowned as she saw Artis just standing on the sidewalk, looking lost and woebegone. She moved quickly towards her, startling Artis from her thoughts.

"Artis? What are you up to?" Daci grinned at her. "I don't think you're standing here just to keep the sidewalk from tripping someone."

"No, I'm not." Artis shook her head to clear her thoughts. "I was headed into the library and then just couldn't go into it."

"That makes sense. The woman that they suspect? She works there." Daci linked an arm with Artis and turned her from that building. "Come with me. I need to pick your brain about some of the youths that are in the shelter." Daci pointed at Artis' car. "Let's get you over there with your car."

Artis nodded, suddenly wanting to be out of sight. She glanced around, not seeing anyone after her but knowing full well that someone was. Aidan had been called in to a crime scene during the night. He had been reluctant to leave her but both of them knew that he had to do what he was required to do.

"That works." Artis was still very uncomfortable, feeling danger approaching her. "Someone is out here, Daci. And they don't mean me any good."

"They don't." Daci snapped her seatbelt closed. "I think that we need to get you to somewhere safe. Head for Don's. We can work there." She had set her briefcase on the car floor.

Artis nodded and drove away, not seeing the cars that pulled out to follow her. Pulling up to Don' building, Artis turned off her car, shifted the gears into park, and then just sat there. She was puzzling through what she knew and not liking what she was thinking.

Don frowned as he heard Daci's voice and peered around his office door. To see Artis with her was disturbing.

"Daci? I thought you were working today." Don waited for the two ladies to approach him.

"I am. I'm working with Artis. She tried to go into the library and couldn't. We both know why that was. Now, we need to go over everything that they have. We stopped by their place and grabbed all that we needed. The guys are done at noon, aren't they?"

"They are. And the ladies are heading our way with a meal." Don sent off a text to Delanie to include enough food for the two ladies. "Aidan's working?"

"He is. He was called in early this morning." Artis paced the hallway. "Can we solve it today, Don, do you think?"

"We can do our best." He looked around as the door opened once more. "Emma? You're here?"

"I am. God told me to come. Abe's outside right now. And I heard that Samuel is heading this way." Emma reached to hug Artis. "We'll work as long as we need to, Artis. Our son is with Abe's aunt. So we don't have that worry."

"Thank you, Emma." Artis frowned at her. "You have more information."

"I do, Artis. I need your parents here as well."

Artis nodded, sending off a text to both her parents and Aidan's. She knew that Aidan's family needed to be involved. A quick response came from both sets of parents that they were on their way. What could they bring with them?

Aidan walked into his home that afternoon, surprised not to find Artis waiting for him. His heart grew fearful until he saw the note on the kitchen counter. He rushed to lock away his police gear and then change to casual clothing. Out of the house, Aidan paused for a moment, lost in thought, before he ran for his truck and headed for Don's. He had not expected this but he should have.

Artis felt an arm around her and looked up, finding Aidan reaching to kiss her before he just held her. His eyes searched the conference room, surprised at the activity that was heated. He could hear the conversation and occasional laughter before his gaze dropped back to Artis.

"Been working, sweetheart?" His voice was low enough that only she could hear him.

"We have been. We've made progress, Aidan. We'll need to pass it all on to George. Emma said that she would. She's been in contact on and off all day." She shifted on her chair to study her groom. "You're exhausted."

"I am. Lyle told me to take tomorrow morning at least, if I needed to. I might. But first, what's the plan here?" He looked around, not surprised to see who all had shown up. "Toryn's here."

"He is. He and Slaney showed up about an hour ago. He told me that he's here as a friend only."

"He would do that. It's who he is." Aidan looked around as silence spread through the room and was not surprised that Gideon was there and on his feet to ask a blessing on their meal.

Abe approached Aidan thirty minutes later, assessing his friend. He was wearing out, Abe decided. Not just from this but from the cases that he's working. He's afraid that he'll bring danger to anyone he approached through his work.

"Aidan?" Abe's voice caught Aidan's attention and he looked at Abe

"Abe? What did you find?"

"A lot. And it means a lot more danger for you two. This is deep into your town. And involves more people than you would expect." Abe bit at his lip for a moment, not quite sure how to proceed with what he needed to say.

"It involves our force, doesn't it?" Aidan didn't need a reply. It was what the consensus had become.

Chapter 37

Aidan's head was bent over the papers that he was reading. He didn't like the names that had been determined to be involved. They were not who he had expected. As he thought through it, Aidan nodded. They were the correct names. He looked around to find Toryn sitting beside him.

"Toryn? Were you expecting this?"

"I was, unfortunately, Aidan. We both know the families involved and the rumours that have circulated over the years about them. How do we now protect you two?" Toryn was worried about his friend.

"I don't know, Toryn. Given the depth that they are involved in this town, I need to step aside as a detective. I'm too dangerous out there. If they go after me, someone else could be hurt."

Toryn nodded. Aidan had gone right to the centre of their dilemma.

"That's true. I talked to Lyle. We need you to keep working. He's assigned trusted officers to be with you. Their sole purpose is to watch out for you, not on what you are doing. Don's team is stepping in with Artis as will Richard and Abe. At night, once you are in and not leaving, patrol officers are outside your home. We won't intrude on you, Aidan. We'll do what we can to make sure that you're safe. And that means that you're not driving yourself anywhere for now."

Aidan nodded, an arm reaching to wrap Artis close to him. She had heard Toryn's words, he knew. He didn't like that his freedom had just walked away from him but he knew the reasons why the steps were being taken.

Late that night, Aidan locked away the paperwork that he had brought home with them. He heard Artis moving quietly around the house and sighed. This was not what he had planned to spend his night. God had had other plans for them. Aidan was thankful for his friends and their willingness to work through what he and Artis were going through.

Artis was awake early in the morning, her thoughts troubled until she began to pray. She felt the peace that only God can give. On her feet and dressed, she headed for the office, retrieved the material, and then sat at the desk. Reading through it all, Artis frowned. They had too much information, she decided, and reached for the computer mouse. Working away, she sorted through a database with everything. Shocked at what she had discovered, she sat back and stared at the computer screen. She then reached to send the material to Emma and George. What they would do with it, she had no idea.

George opened the email a couple of hours later. He read through what Artis had forwarded to him and frowned. He didn't understand how she had reached her conclusions but she was correct. She had pinpointed the person responsible and it was not who they had expected at all.

Aidan paused beside Artis, tilting his head to study her face. She's discovered something, he decided, and isn't sure how to proceed.

"What did you find, sweetheart?" Aidan knelt beside her chair and wrapped her in a hug.

"This. This is the person. I just sorted through everything we did yesterday. I sent it to Emma and George. What do we do, Aidan?"

Aidan's gaze shifted to the computer monitor and read as Artis scrolled through the pages for him. He frowned at the person who she had pinpointed. Aidan nodded.

"You're correct with this, sweetheart. Now, we need to stay safe and I'm not sure that we can." He sighed before he was on his feet and drawing Artis to hers. "Let's eat and then spend time in prayer. We need that time in prayer, sweetheart. This is where it gets more dangerous for us."

"I know. Now, we need to make some plans. I won't stay home, Aidan. I want this over. This means that we go on the offensive."

"It does. We need to make plans." Aidan paused as he worked away on their breakfast. His thoughts were troubled, to say the least. Now, Artis wanted to be out there and hunting for those responsible for what they were going through. He had second thoughts about that but he had to admit that he agreed with her

Artis buried her head in her hands. She was exhausted, her sleep troubled by nightmares, the worse of them being that Aidan disappeared forever or was killed in her presence. She shuddered for a moment before she looked up at him.

"Aidan, what are your thoughts?"

"You are correct with your thoughts. That person is the one behind it. They are out in the open all the time. No one would suspect them. Now, we need to make plans as to how we move forward without putting ourselves in greater danger."

"That's the risk, isn't it?" Artis rubbed at the wooden table top. "I don't want anyone else to be hurt. But I know that they will be. How do we stop that from happening?"

"I don't know, but I know that our friends will work with us on that." Aidan grew pensive. This was definitely not how he expected to start off his married life. In fact, he had had no plans to marry. He turned his attention to his bride, knowing that they needed to be out an about but deeply afraid for her. "We can't continue to hide, sweetheart."

"No, we can't. It won't solve this if we do. So how do we do this without endangering anyone else?"

"We go out and live life. We take all the precautions that we can. God is in control, sweetheart. He has us in the hollow of His hand. We need to look up and see how He protects us."

"I know, my love, but it is hard to do that. I just want this over." Artis sighed as she rose to clear off the table. "You're working this afternoon?"

"I am. I'm in the office. I can take you with me, if you like. You can curl up in a chair in my office and work on what you want to." Aidan rose as well, heading for the door. He opened it to find Lyle standing there. "Lyle?"

"In the house, Aidan." Lyle's voice and face were grim. "I saw what Artis sent George. He's already confirmed her thoughts. That person is here in your neighbourhood and has been stalking you two."

Artis peered around Aidan, seeing that Lyle was angry.

"They have been? I knew that I was being watched constantly. That explains it."

Chapter 38

That afternoon, Aidan and Artis boldly walked away from the police department building and headed for the downtown area, their hands joined. Artis was afraid. This was not how she had thought that they would step out in faith but apparently the powers-that-be had decided that they should. She knew that there were officers in plain clothes around them but it didn't make her feel any safer.

Aidan's eyes were on the move, watching for anyone who might approach them. He sighed as well. This was a plan that they had come up with, desperate as Aidan was to draw out their protagonist. He just didn't like putting Artis in the line of fire. Not that she would be anywhere else. If he was out there, she bluntly told him, then she would be out there as well.

The man following the couple didn't care that there were officers around them. He had fully expected that. He was patient. He would wait until the opportunity presented itself. Then, he would act as quickly as he could. He turned and walked away, not seeing George following him.

Aidan pulled Artis into a store and then through it and out of the back door. She stared at him, not sure why he had done what he had.

"Aidan?"

"We're being followed, Artis. I hope that by doing this, we've managed to escape them." He stared at her before he tugged at her hand. He frowned as she didn't move. "Artis?"

"We're not going anywhere on our own, Aidan." She nodded towards the men standing behind him. "We have company."

Aidan turned cautiously, his heart dropping as he saw the men standing there. They were the men who had kidnapped them the first time. His hands were raised as a weapon was pointed at them.

"Aidan?" Artis' hand was on his back. She wasn't sure what to do. She was relying on Artis to lead.

"We'll need to go with them, sweetheart. We don't have much choice." Aidan walked forward before one of the men stopped him and pulled his hands behind him. He felt handcuffs click around his wrists and heard the whimper from Artis as she was handcuffed as well. They were both shoved into a truck before the three men were in it as well and the truck was speeding off.

The officers following them slid to a stop, consternation on their faces. They had not expected Aidan to make the move that he did. They had been moments behind him and lost sight of him.

"Where is he?" George spun in a circle, not seeing either one of the couple.

"They're gone, George." The older patrol officer nodded towards the end of the alleyway. "I saw the end of a truck disappearing when we came out."

"They've been taken. Then, we need to find them." George spun in another circle, searching the buildings. "There. We have video surveillance." He was on the run for the store, startling the worker. "I need to see your video feed."

The worker stared at him before heading for the office. George leaned close as the worker pulled up the feed. He searched it, asking that it be paused.

"I need a copy of that feed. That's a kidnapping." George took the thumb drive that was handed to him. He headed outside to find Lyle heading for him.

"George? Is it true?"

"It is. I have the evidence of their kidnapping as well as clear photos of the men and their truck. I've put out the description of the truck and its plate number. I pray that we find them soon."

"Me, too." Lyle looked around. "Were there any witnesses?"

"No. It was totally empty at the time. It's like it was planned." George was frustrated at that. "I'm heading back to see what I can find out." He walked away, pausing as he slid behind the wheel of his car. He didn't like what had happened. All George could do at the moment was to pray for his friends.

Alin turned from the door of his house, allowing Lyle and Toryn to enter. He feared that they were there. His hand reached for Ardeen's before he pointed to the living room. Bayne was on his feet, a hand resting on Bridy's shoulders. The parents had been meeting for Bible study and prayer and had not expected to see the two officers who had appeared.

"Toryn? Lyle? You're here for a reason." Ardeen's face paled. "Just tell us. Are they alive?"

"We believe that they are. They disappeared about an hour ago from the down town. We have a description of the men and the truck but no signs of them."

Ardeen sank into her chair, horror on her face. This is what had been expected but they had prayed that it would never happen.

"What happened, Toryn?" Bayne's arm was around his wife, sitting beside her on the couch.

"They were down town and disappeared through a store and then into an alleyway. They disappeared into a truck and then from the alleyway. We're working on finding them." Toryn's tone was grim.

"I see." Bayne began to pray out loud, begging for the lives of their children. His prayers were picked up by the others. When he finished, he paused for a moment before he raise his head. His face and eyes had hardened. "What can we do to find them, Toryn?"

"We need to go over some material with you. George has it. We would ask that you come to the office to do that." Toryn rose, watching as the two sets of parents surged to their feet and headed for the door. He shared a look with Lyle, who simply shrugged, a small grin on his face.

George turned from the table in the conference room that he had taken over, spreading out all of the paperwork on the tables. He had other officers working with him to go through it all. The whiteboards were filling up with information as a buzz of conversation in turn filled up the room.

"What do you need from us?" Bridy took the initiative and went right went to the point.

"I need you to go through what we have. Alin, you and Ardeen know the town. Bayne and Bridy, you know your town. Somehow this is connected between the towns." George stepped back out into the hallway, watching their movements. He turned as Lyle stopped beside him.

"George?"

"They're already digging in to the paperwork, Lyle. They won't leave until they come to some conclusion. I know that it's unorthodox to do this but we have to find some common ground. We'll verify what they know. That's a given. The police board had given the green light for this. It's not what we normally do."

"No, it's not. You have given them only certain paperwork that would be available to them any way. What we need to keep confidential you've done." Lyle watched for a few moments before he walked away. There were other duties that he needed to be about but his prayer was for George and his team and then for Aidan and Artis.

Chapter 39

Early the next morning, George rose from his chair, yawned, and then stretched. He looked around the room, noting that cots had been brought in and that both sets of parents were asleep, or at least he thought that they were. He walked around the perimeter of the room, reading the whiteboards. He nodded as he read the information there. They were closer to where they needed to be but there was one crucial piece of information that was missing. George had no idea what it was.

Bayne had been watching George and then rose to stand beside him.

"George? You're troubled."

"I am, Bayne. We need that one crucial piece of information that we don't have to prove who it is. And we don't have it." George rubbed at his face.

Bayne nodded. He had come to the same conclusion. He wanted this over for his daughter and her groom. He wanted them home. Bayne just didn't know when they would come home and what condition that they would be in.

"I get that, George. How do we find it?" Bayne walked away, reading the boards. He wasn't supposed to but George didn't have the heart to stop him. It might mean trouble when they went to court but they would deal with that as they had to. Toryn had taken the unusual step of swearing in the four as officers, just for the duration. The police board had been behind him on that.

George walked over to where Bayne had paused. Bayne's finger rested on a name. George frowned at it.

"Bayne? This person is from your town."

"He is. He's always puzzled me. He never seemed to have a source of income." Bayne looked past George at Alin as he stood nearby. "Alin?"

"I know that name, Bayne. He's related to someone here in town." Alin frowned at the board. "I can't remember the name, though."

Bayne said a name, his eyes on Alin. Alin stopped rubbing at his face and then nodded.

"That's him. How do you prove it, George?" Alin turned to the younger man.

"By digging deep." His phone was out as he sent off a text to Emma. He knew that she would dig deep. He paused for a moment. "That friend of yours, Alin?"

"Samuel? He had information on that man." Alin was sorting through paperwork and then held up a file. "Here. He had information on that man, without knowing the connection."

George reached for the file, his eyes shifting between the two fathers. His eyes dropped to the paperwork as he read it. He looked around, pulled out a chair, and sat, the folder on the table in front of him.

Alin and Bayne moved away, their eyes on the young detective.

“Will this solve it, do you think, Alin?” Bayne prayed that it would.

“I pray that it does. We need to find our kids. I wish this hadn’t happened, but God has allowed it. I know that God is in control. It’s hard to trust at times like this.”

“It is, very hard.” Bayne turned to study Bridy as she slept. “This is taking a lot from our wives.”

“It is. Bayne? Come with me.” Alin walked away, heading for the outdoors through the front of the building. “I need some fresh air. Let’s walk for a bit and then find us some breakfast.”

“We can do that.” Bayne’s head went back as he looked up, his eyes taking in the lightening of the sky as dawn crept in. “What can we do to bring this to a conclusion?”

“Call in Don, Richard, and Abe. And call Samuel and his crew.” Alin was adamant about that. “They all have resources that we can use. I know that George will work away on what he can but he has to prove it all before he can make a move.”

Bayne was nodding as Alin spoke before his phone was out. He was sending out text message after text message, not waiting for any response. He leaned against a building wall as Alin walked away. His thoughts were troubled.

Alin returned, a bag of food in his hand. He waited patiently as Alin responded to his text messages.

"We're set, Alin. Let's eat and then take our ladies to Don's place. We're meeting there in two hours. Abe and Richard were already on their way to there." Bayne shoved away from the wall, not feeling the hand that reached into his jacket pocket and dropped a piece of paper into it before the young boy was running away.

Bayne was puzzled two hours later as he shoved his hands into his pockets. They had gathered at Don's and spent time in prayer before Bayne rose and walked away. He was pacing the outside, Nathaniel from Abe's team and Timothy from Richard's team with him. Bayne frowned at the piece of paper.

Nathaniel reached for it with gentle fingers and took it from Bayne's hand. He read it and then passed it to Timothy.

"Bayne? When did you get that?" Nathaniel's words broke through the stillness of the fall day.

"I don't know. It must have been when Alin and I were outside earlier. I didn't feel anyone putting it there." He frowned at the two men. "Is it for real?"

"We'll look into it." Timothy was running for the building, the piece of paper clenched in his hands.

"He'll talk with Emma and her crew. Samuel will look into it as well." Nathaniel's eyes were in constant motion. "Someone is watching us."

"Of course they are. They want to see how distraught you are. And none of us are showing that. God has placed His peace in our hearts. We are worried and scared for sure, but we have to acknowledge that God is in control and that He only wants the best. It's hard to trust in situations like this but we must. Even just the smallest bit of faith is all it takes." Bayne sighed, his head dropping for a moment. "It doesn't mean that we have to like what we or our families go through. You understand that only too well, Nathaniel."

"Unfortunately, all our team members know that. You have heard our stories. You have heard how God used us to bring someone to justice. Murphy also maintains that God has a plan and purpose for our lives that we don't know or understand. That's what faith is." Nathaniel's hand rested on Bayne's shoulder. "We know how tough it is to wait. God will avenge your kids. We know that."

"Thank you, Nathaniel. Your words help. You speak from experience, unfortunately. Thank you for being here." Bayne wiped at his eyes, unable to contain his emotions for a moment.

"We would be nowhere else, Bayne. It's who we are. We are God's hands and feet on earth. This is one way that we can do that. And we won't walk away until they are home. Even afterwards, we will be there for them to speak with, cry with. God takes that from us. He expects us to come to Him as we would our earthly daddies. He takes any and all emotions that we throw at him."

Bayne had been listening closely to Nathaniel as he spoke. His arm had come out to wrap around Bridy as she had come to find him and drew her close to him. He could feel her nodding against him.

"That is so true, Nathaniel." Bridy spoke for the two of them. "You have put it so well. We have to trust Him with Aidan and Artis. It's just hard to give up control and do that."

"It is hard, Bridy." Elizabeth, Nathaniel's wife, had approached as well. "As humans, we need to be in control. It is hard to surrender our will to His."

The two couples stood for a moment before Nathaniel pointed to the building, anxious to get the older couple inside and out of sight. He turned to watch the road, seeing the car drive away. His feelings were correct. Someone had been observing them.

Chapter 40

Bayne stared at Abe as he spoke rapidly. Was he really saying that they knew where Alin and Artis were?

"What did you say?" Bayne's hand was out to rest on Abe's shoulders. "Did you really say that you know where they are?" Hope was rising in the older man's heart.

"We're fairly sure, Bayne. Some of us are heading that way. It's a public building at that so we don't have to worry about trespassing." Abe was away, taking Murphy and Matt from his team. Richard and Naomi followed him as did Paul and Caleb from Don's team.

Bayne prayed that they were correct and that they would find the younger couple. He didn't know how long that Bridy would be able to function and hold up. He knew that she was deeply worried as were Alin and Ardeen. He drew Bridy back to his side and went to find Alin and Ardeen. That couple were in the kitchen of the building, working with Daci and Melanie on a meal.

Alin turned as he felt Bayne's hand on his shoulder, a frown on his face that turn to hope.

"Bayne?"

"Abe thinks that he knows where they are. They are heading out to the building that they have centred their attention on. We need to pray for them." Bayne felt hope rising in his heart that their children would be home that day.

"They do? That doesn't surprise me. Abe has done this before." Alin looked around. "We need to gather together and pray for them." He dropped the loaf of bread that he was holding and reached for Ardeen's hand. They walked rapidly to the conference room followed by the others. The meal preparation was forgotten for the moment.

Abe sent the men in one by one before he followed them. He looked around. The library of all places, he thought. Of course, this place held thousands of stories. He just didn't expect that it would be part of Aidan's and Artis'.

Richard stood beside him, his eyes searching the staff. He drew a quick breath of relief. The person that was suspected to be involved in this kidnapping was not there. He pointed towards a hallway and walked that way, Abe at his side. He heard the quiet footsteps following him and knew that the others were there.

"Richard? Would they be on this floor or the basement?" Abe kept his voice low. He felt his phone vibrate and pulled it out to squint at the message. "Emma's tracked them to the basement."

"How?" Richard waved his hand. He knew well how she had managed that. One of them had a tracking device on them and had been able to active it. He suspected that it was Artis who had it. It was something that Abe had done before, particularly for his team member, Luke, and his lady, Abi.

Richard pointed towards a door and walked that way. He pulled open the door, finding the lights on. That was good news. The group walked down the steps as quietly as they could and began to search. Abe still had his phone in his hand, following Emma's texts. He paused in front of a door and pointed.

Richard nodded, his hand reaching for the key that was still in the lock. He had no hesitation in doing so. Caleb was a member of the library board and could justify them being there. He prayed as he reached for the door knob and twisted it. The door opened, surprisingly not squeaking. Richard, Matt, Naomi, and Paul entered the room, searching it before Matt gave a sound and sprang forward. He was on his knees beside Aidan, hands reaching to assess him.

"He's alive, but he's been beaten." Matt twisted on his knees, seeing Naomi on her knees beside Artis. "Naomi?"

"She's alive, Matt. We need to get them out of here." She stood as Caleb reached to gather Artis into his arms.

Aidan was dropped to his feet and then draped over Murphy's shoulder. The group moved quietly away, Richard pausing to lock the door once more. Caleb nodded towards the stairs near them.

"Up there. It takes us to the back parking lot. I just pray that no one is there." He waited at the foot of the stairs as Paul and Murphy ran up them and carefully opened the door. The two men shared a look. The door opened right at their vehicles. They had not known that but God had. He had directed them where to park. The group moved quickly to sort themselves out in the vehicles before heading for the hospital.

Abe had his phone back out, turning it over and over. He was torn. He needed to let the parents know that the couple was safe but he also needed to let the authorities know. Calling George won the toss in his mind.

"George?" Abe could hear quiet noise in the background. "Can you talk?"

George rose from the table in the conference room where he had his paperwork spread out and walked to a corner. He stood there and watched the harried and hurried activity in the room.

"I can, Abe. What do you need?" George heard a softly indrawn breath and frowned.

"We have them, George. We're on the way to the hospital with them." Abe waited someway impatiently for George to respond.

George stared across the room before he was running from it, heading to find Lyle and then Toryn.

"You have them?" George could barely get his words out.

"We do. They were locked in a room in the basement of the library. We had Caleb with us and as a board member, he can go anywhere there. You'll need to get your search warrant for the last room on the right in the basement. They were locked in there."

"How are they?" George's hand reached out to stop Lyle from moving away from him.

Lyle frowned at George before he turned and waved Toryn over. That man frowned at George as well.

"They're unconscious. Aidan has been beaten." Abe ducked his head to stare at the hospital. "We're at the hospital. You need to get their parents here." Abe tucked his phone away into a pocket, ignoring George's questions.

"George?" Toryn continued to frown at him.

"Abe and the others have Aidan and Artis. They're at the hospital with them." George studied the two men with him. "I need to work on a search warrant. Someone needs to be there. And someone needs to find their parents."

Toryn reached for his car keys.

"Lyle, you're with them. George, pull in whoever it is that you need. I would suggest speaking with Emma. I'm off to find the parents."

Don looked up from where he had been studying the driveway, surprised to find Toryn walking towards him.

"Toryn?"

"Where are their parents?" Toryn gave a short nod at the question on Don's face. He followed Don into the conference room, finding both sets of parents on their feet and moving his way. "We have them. Abe called George. We need to get you to the hospital." He gave a grim smile at the look of disbelief on the other couples' faces before they were running for the door, some members from each team with them.

Chapter 41

The parents sorted themselves out in the waiting room, impatient to see their children. They didn't understand how Aidan and Artis had been found but they were grateful that they had been. They all knew that God had been there in directly the team who had gone in. Each of the parents had found each one of the team and hugged them. Ardeen and Bridy could not control their tears.

Lyle waited somewhat impatiently in the hallway outside Aidan's room. There were officers assigned to the door but he also knew that Richard was with Aidan and that a lady named Naomi was with Artis. He didn't take any steps to remove their guards. It appeared that they needed all the protection that they could have with them.

Toryn approached, a frown on his face. He felt that as all he was doing lately.

"What's the word?" His keen gaze studied the lead detective.

"Artis has been awake. She had given up, she said. George was around and took her statement. He's in with Aidan at the moment. Artis wasn't hurt. Aidan was beaten somewhat. Artis said that was when he tried to protect her. She asked if it was over. I think it is almost."

"It is. I spoke with George. He served the search warrant and sent in a team. The men and ladies are fighting mad, he tells me." Toryn gave a quick grin at the snort that Lyle permitted himself. "It's been enough for our force, Lyle. I pray that no one else goes through this."

"You and me both." He looked around. "You need to speak with their parents."

"I have already. They are overwhelmed right now. Once they can get back here to see them, then we'll sort them out to where we need them."

"I would suggest that we take them out of town for the next couple of days. Richard and Abe have offered their places. I would suggest Abe's. He has the cabins that he uses for events like these."

"I won't go anywhere." Artis stood in front of the two officers, a fierce look on her face. "I will not be chased from my home." She spun on her heel and almost ran to find Aidan.

Lyle began to snicker, Toryn joining him once his shock had worn off.

"I guess that we got told. Let me know how this resolves." Toryn walked away, needing to be at a meeting that he really didn't want to be at.

Lyle stepped into the room, finding George waiting for him. George grinned at him.

"Not going how you planned?"

Lyle shook his head. He knew Aidan well enough to know that he would choose the same as Artis.

"We'll make sure that they have protection but they are not willing to leave town." Lyle walked away after a few moments. He would catch up with Aidan later.

That afternoon, Aidan stretched out on the couch, his head on Artis' lap. He slept, feeling safe for the first time in weeks. George had been around again, just to bring them up to date on the investigation. They had begun the process of serving arrest and search warrants, working up the chain to the top. He had officers watching that person. If that person made any attempt to flee, they would be apprehended and held.

Artis was not as confident as her groom. She had studied George before walking away despite his protest that she stay and hear what he had to say. She was hiding, she knew, and shouldn't. She had just had enough.

Ardeen and Bridy were in the kitchen, deeply worried about their children. They didn't say much but then again, they didn't have to. Alin and Bayne were with Don and his team, trying to come up a plan for the next few days.

Artis was trying hard to remember all the verses and Scripture passages that she and Aidan had been studying the last few weeks. She couldn't and that drove her to tears. Her emotions were all over the place. She felt Aidan's hand tightening on hers and knew that he sensed her distress even while asleep. Artis frowned at Toryn as he took a seat across from her, his eyes closing for a moment as he prayed for his friends.

"Toryn? How close are we to solving this and letting us live our lives?" Artis' voice was low. She had been almost afraid to ask him.

"We're getting there, Artis. We're working up the chain of command. I have officers watching the one who we think is in charge." Toryn was just afraid that they were looking at the wrong person.

"Is it Judy Watts?" Artis had come across that name in her research and had asked Aidan about her. He had stared at her before he nodded. Artis had named the one person that they had not looked at but should have.

"Where did you come up with that name?" Toryn was surprised. He had not considered her at all. His phone was out as he sent a text message to both George and Lyle, knowing that George had considered her and then set her aside.

"She was there. Aidan didn't see her but I did. I recognized her from her photo. I wanted to go into the library one day and just couldn't. The sense of evil was just so great. God does that, doesn't He?"

"Does what?" Toryn frowned at her.

"Stop us from entering places that mean danger to us."

"He does, Artis. He does." Toryn watched as Aidan roused and sat up to wrap Artis in his arms. "We have all experienced that at some point."

"You know, when we were locked up, I saw Gabe and Mike. They were in the room with us but didn't say anything." Artis was thinking that through.

"God sends us angels to protect us. I think that Gabe and Mike are ours. I have felt their presence at times but haven't seen them."

"They have been around us, sweetheart." Aidan had felt their presence as well.

"He does that." Toryn looked around as he heard the doorbell and was on his feet, heading that way. His hands rose at the weapon pointed at him before he backed away. He didn't hear the steps behind him before the butt of a weapon crashed down on his head, seeing him to the floor. He didn't hear Artis' scream or see that the mothers had been removed from the house and locked into Aidan's garden shed.

Judy Watts stared down at Toryn's still body with distain. If he died, it would be no loss to her. In fact, she could then work to put in a police chief who would bend to her will. She didn't realize that the officers who were looking for her had been alerted to the fact that she was at Aidan's.

Aidan sensed danger and looked up. He sank back on the couch as he saw Watts appearing in his living room. His arm tightened around Artis. Aidan felt her shifting and glanced down at her. Her face was without expression.

"Well, well, well. At last, I have you exactly where I want you, McNeill. And your woman? She's here as well." She sneered at them as she walked heavily across the floor. Her lifestyle had led to her become overweight but she didn't care. She just continued with her love of liquor, wine, and rich food.

"What did we ever do to you?" Aidan's voice was calm despite the tumult and fear that he was feeling.

"What did you ever do to me? Nothing. Absolutely nothing." She sneered at him once more.

"Then, why? I don't understand why you would hate us this much." Artis frowned at her before her face cleared. "Joe Watts." Her memory had finally recognized the connection between her town and Aidan's. "He's related to you."

"He is. He was adopted by my sister but you took him from her."

"No, I had nothing to do with that. He walked away from her abuse. I spoke with him briefly one day on the street but I had nothing to do with his leaving." Artis shifted closer to Aidan.

"He walked through this town one day." Aidan remembered the youth and had been troubled at what Joe had told him when they had spoken. Aidan had found Joe on the street and shared a meal at Ben's with him. Joe had disappeared shortly after. Aidan wondered where the young man was now. That had been about four years ago, if his memory was correct.

"You should have stopped him. I saw you talking with him that day and expected you to keep him here in town. My sister would have been here to get him." Watts was growing increasingly angry. She could hear the three men who were with her shifting on their feet. She jut didn't realize that they didn't want any part of this. They hadn't been the ones who had kidnapped Aidan or Artis either time.

"Sorry. That's not how it works. He was free to live how he wanted to. He had committed no crimes."

"He was sixteen. He should have been with his parents. And you should have done that."

Aidan shrugged, knowing that no matter what he said, it would not pacify her.

"I had no idea how old he was. Even at sixteen, he can live on his own. There was nothing for me to do to keep him here." Aidan's eyes narrowed as he heard soft movement in the house. He just prayed that they were friends here to help and not more of her men. His heart cried out to God for protection for his lady and their mothers. He wondered where those ladies were.

"No, you were to stop him." Watts had pulled a weapon from the mammoth and gaudy purse that she had on her arm. She peered at him and then at Artis. She wanted to shoot them but she didn't know which one to shoot first. She didn't hear the cautious footsteps that were approaching her from behind. Watts screamed as a hand caught her arm in a hard, tight grasp and pointed the weapon to the ceiling. Another hand reached to grip her hand and remove the weapon from it.

Handcuffs were snapped around her wrists despite her struggles. Her struggles against the officers took her to the floor where they had a great difficulty subduing her. Hauled to her feet, Watts screamed at Aidan and Artis and then at the officers. She resisted being removed from the house. George and Lyle stood and watched as she struggled against being shoved into a patrol car. Her vile shouts and cursing filled the night air, bringing neighbours out to see what the commotions.

Toryn was on his feet, shaking off any help offered him. With a hand to his head pressing against the lump, he staggered for a moment before he found a seat in the living room once more. He stared at the couple who were staring back at him.

"Toryn? Are you okay?" Artis was worried about her friend.

"I will be. Now, what about you two?"

"We are." Aidan looked up as their mothers rushed into the room. "Mom? Bridy?"

"We're fine, Aidan. We were locked in your garden shed. I think we made a bit of a mess trying to get out."

"Not a problem, Mom." Aidan was on his feet to hug the two ladies who then hugged Artis.

"Have we solved this?" Bridy sat beside her daughter, not wanting to leave her.

"We have, Mom. We have. All because someone wanted her adopted nephew not to leave home and blamed us for that. I don't blame him for leaving. I know who his adopted parents are. They are into crime, if I remember correctly, and were arrested a year or so ago." Artis yawned. "I'm tired." The rush of adrenalin had faded and left her exhausted.

Late that night, Aidan reached to tuck Artis close to him. They had retired but not to sleep. Artis' emotions were still to muddled for her to relax enough to sleep. Aidan felt the same way. He just began to pray for them both and for God to grant them restorative sleep. They were soon asleep, not hearing the footsteps of the officers who circled the house, still on watch for their friend and his bride.

George stood and watched as Judy Watts was interrogated. She was drifting into a state that gave concern for her mental health. They would need to have that evaluated before they could go on with their interrogation. Toryn stood beside him.

"No one would have ever thought that she was capable of kidnapping and attempted murder." Toryn was thinking that through. "She presented herself as a competent and caring member of our community."

"She did. I've been looking into her. She seemed to go off the sanity rails when her nephew ran away from home and then when her sister and husband were arrested, that seemed to send her all the way over the edge. I doubt that we will ever get her to trial."

"Not likely. Take tomorrow, George. Don't come in. You have done great work in this. God is working in our lives and this is part of it. He has led all the way in this investigation, even when we were struggling."

"He did, Toryn." George finally moved away from the window, yawning as he glanced at his watch. He would set aside what he was working on and then come back fresh on the morrow. It was now after midnight.

Aidan was on a search two months later. It was a Saturday morning and he was looking for his bride. He stopped for a moment to watch as she worked away on the front porch, decorating it for the Christmas season. It was early December and she had plans that she wanted to put into place.

Artis looked up as she felt watched, not afraid this time. She walked quickly into Aidan's arms and returned his hug. He was someone who loved to hug and she had come to expect that. Artis looked up at him, seeing his love for her shining on his face.

"Aidan? What are you up to?"

"I want to take my bride out for a meal. Ready to eat, sweetheart?"

Artis shrugged. He was up to something more than just a meal.

"What are you up to? It's more than that."

Aidan shrugged. Ben had called him and told him that he had a meal ready for them. They just needed to show up.

"No, Ben asked that we come for a meal. I have no idea why."

Artis sighed. She had finished with the front porch and had just wanted to take it easy. It didn't seem as if that would happen.

"Just let me get cleaned up and we can go."

Aidan tidied away the boxes from her decorating and then reached to hug Artis once more as she approached him, grateful that God had chosen Artis to be his bride.

Walking into Ben's a short while later, Aidan's steps faltered and then stopped. He looked around, hearing Artis' soft whisper. Their friends and families were there.

Ben approached the young couple, hugging them and then stepping back.

"We wanted to do something to help you celebrate your wedding. You didn't have that. We decided as a group to do this. If we have overstepped, forgive us."

Artis simply hugged him again before she wiped away tears of happiness. The couple moved among the people gathered, receiving and giving hugs. It was hours before the group finally dispersed.

Aidan stood in their living room, his eyes on his bride.

"Artis?" He moved towards her, wrapping her into a hug. "Did you expect this?"

"Absolutely not. Did you?" She smiled as he shook his head. "We have a great group of friends here in Oak City and then from the other towns. We need to do something for them."

"And we will. For now, we'll discuss what we want to do and then make plans." His chin rested on the top of her head. "What are you thinking?"

"Did you see Gabe and Mike there?"

"No, I missed them. I would have liked to talk with them."

"They were there and then gone. I am convinced that they are angels."

"It is highly possible, sweetheart. Now, as for you? What are your plans?"

"For work? Daci has asked me to step in with the shelter when I need to. I like that flexibility. I was burnt out and I think that's why I quit."

"That's fine, sweetheart." Aidan stared down at her head. "I love you so much, Artis. You are the one I was waiting all my life for." He kissed her and then kissed her again.

Artis smiled up at him before she reached to kiss him.

"You are the image of the knights that Mom put into my bedtime stories. God brought us together at the time that He was ready for us to meet. I don't like what we had to go through but He was there every step of the way. He gave us His peace through it all. I couldn't have managed without that. He knew before time began what we would face and how we would face it."

"He did, sweetheart. I had a long talk with Gideon the other day. He said the same thing. In fact, he is planning on a series of sermons on that topic."

"And we will understand so much better having gone through it."

Thank you for choosing the story of Aidan and his lady, Artis. He has been vocal about having a story to tell and wouldn't let me rest until I told it. Artis was to have been named Cavanagh but like the ladies before her, she rebelled at that name. The names that I choose reflect the Irish heritage that comes through my maternal side of the family. The paternal side is English.

As to what this couple faced, they were in difficult stressful work. Burn out is common in these forms of employment. The stress causes illness of all ilks. They depended on God to bring them through safely and to provide the peace that only He can give.

To have that peace of God is precious. He is willing to take any emotion that we throw at Him. He is our Abba Father and doesn't want us to hide from Him what He already knows we feel and face. A character in a previous novel, Richard, said that we need come to our beloved Father as a child would his fatherly father. He never failed to close off a pray with "I love you". How many times do we say that to God? There are times we take Him for granted and move ahead in our lives without waiting on Him.

This doesn't end the stories of the characters who live in Oak City. There are others clambering for their stories to be told as there are from other towns. We'll see who is next.

Now, my unruly characters like to walk back and forth through the stories. Toryn and Slaney's story is

Toryn. Abe's team is *His Guardians.* Doug and Darcy's is *The Heart of a Lion.* Richard's team is *His Protectors.* Don's team is *His Defenders.* Jacob, Blackie, Josh, and Simon share their stories in *Mistletoe* Treasures. Bill and Cora's is *Hidden in the Hollow.* Andrew and Phoebe's is *The Potter's Hands.* Silas and Madigan's is *Strong Courage.* They always help to move the stories along. I don't mind. I miss the characters once their stories are complete.

May God richly bless you as you seek Him and learn to trust in Him. May you find His peace.

And Gabe and Mike. Yes, they were angels, sent by God to protect Artis and Aidan. I strongly believe that we have angels in our daily walk.

Ronna

9 781999 882129 7